Out of Play

A Novel by
Joy Norstrom

CROOKED
CAT

First Crooked Love Cats Edition
Crooked Cat Publishing Ltd. 2016

Discover us online:
www.crookedcatpublishing.com

Join us on facebook:
www.facebook.com/crookedcatpublishing

*Tweet a photo of yourself holding
this book to @crookedcatbooks
and something nice will happen.*

This one's for Diane
who told me 'keep writing.'

Acknowledgements

I am out of words when it comes to expressing my gratitude. So many people have encouraged me on this journey and I can't believe how blessed I've been for your friendship and steadfast support. You know who you are, and I owe you all a very large glass of wine.

To my dear SAWG writing comrades: I am forever grateful we met. Brandi for your joyous enthusiasm, Don for your steadfast beta reading and title production, Jacqueline for walking beside me every single step of the way—your focused energy and late night chats made this journey very special indeed. And to James, who introduced me to the whole concept of larp. Thank you for teaching me what it means to truly immerse oneself into a story.

I would also like to thank Tanis, who guided me through the revision process. I am so thankful for your contributions in getting Out of Play ready to query.

To my mother who filled our home with books and story. Thank you for planting the writing seed and nurturing it with research trips to Viking village re-enactments. I'm sorry we did not find you a boyfriend.

To Crooked Cat: I am inspired by the spirit of collaboration and connection you intentionally foster between authors. To be part of the cat's cradle is to be 'in community,' and I couldn't ask for a better home. A special thank you to Laurence and to Miriam: Your patient guidance and keen eye are a constant blessing.

And to my family: I could not ask for a more loyal and affirming team. You are more than I deserve. Kris, Mia and Jeanie—you are out of this world amazing and I love you.

About the Author

Joy Norstrom is a Canadian coffee addict. She also happens to be the author of *Out of Play*, a women's fiction novel long on humour and short on romance. She enjoys hiking with family, wine with friends and reading late into the wee hours when she should be asleep.

A social worker by trade, Joy also writes short stories about lives in transition. Whether she is championing inclusion, parenting her kidlets or popping into the local coffee shop, she can generally be found engaged in conversation. Why? She believes human connection and laughter keep her grounded in a muddled world.

You can connect with Joy via: **www.joynorstrom.ca**

Out of Play

Chapter One

"So, Gillian, I'm hearing you say you aren't happy. Correct?"

Dr Celeste Torres, my therapist for all of forty-five minutes, looked at me over the top of her purple reading glasses. The designer frames balanced on the tip of her nose, and I had an urge to reach over and push them up. I held myself back.

Certainly the most significant relationship of my life was more complex than not being happy. Wasn't it? But I nodded anyway. "Correct."

Perhaps I'd wasted my money. Not only was her analysis entirely unilluminating, but I was also still clueless how to make my situation any better. Torres looked down at her notes, and I took the opportunity to glance at the oversized wall clock. Ten minutes left.

"And you're telling me that you've explained your unhappiness to Ralph several times? That, basically, every time you see him, you bring up the topic of how much time he spends," Torres stopped mid-sentence and referred to her notes, "live-action roleplaying, or 'larping,' and you express your opinion that he's choosing this activity over you. You tell him how ridiculous and embarrassing you find it that he runs about the woods on a monthly basis pretending to be some fantastical character. Essentially, you have this conversation several times a week. Is this also correct?"

"Yes." I nodded. "Exactly." Perhaps I'd been too quick to judge her. I leaned forward, ready for some expert advice, because I'd already done everything I could. Repeatedly. Trying to talk sense into Ralph had gotten us exactly nowhere. We obviously needed a professional.

When I'd first noticed Dr Torres's advertisement on my Facebook sidebar – *Results. Solutions to all your communication hurdles.* – I'd been curious. But the fact that three of my acquaintances had "liked" her services is what convinced me to pick up the phone and make an appointment. It seemed, after all, a good sign that none of them were divorced.

Granted, only one had ever been married.

"You agree, then," I said. "Ralph and his larp addiction. It's a problem."

Torres leaned back in her desk chair while I teetered on the edge of my overstuffed burgundy armchair, awaiting her expertise on my life.

"Actually, Gillian, I'm not agreeing or disagreeing. I'm only trying to establish the facts. I want to make sure I understand what you're saying." She again looked down at her notes and circled some vague squiggling as I closed my gaping jaw. Not agreeing? How could someone not agree? "I also hear that you and Ralph no longer enjoy activities together. That the time you spend together is usually in a heated discussion about what is wrong with your marriage."

"Absolutely. I just don't see a marriage sustaining itself this way."

"And by not enjoying activities together," she continued as though I hadn't spoken, "I assume this applies to your sexual relationship as well?"

"Oh, er, you know." I blushed. I could feel my embarrassment immediately rising on my face, and knew it was probably outshining the smattering of freckles across the bridge of my nose. "It's not, well, frequent."

She jotted down another note, and I squinted my eyes to try to see what she was writing. No luck. Her scrawl was as much a mystery to me as how to effectively straighten my stubborn brown curls with a flat iron.

This time I didn't even bother to be nonchalant as I glanced at the clock. Five minutes. Five minutes to impart some sanity-saving, marriage-saving wisdom. I had my doubts that would be possible.

Torres took her time folding her hands together atop her notes before addressing me again. "Can I assign you some homework?"

"Yes, of course," I said. "That's why I'm here. I'm committed to finding the solution to this. To making Ralph see the problem."

But there was no rushing her. Another awkward pause ensued, and I could practically hear her wall clock ticking out the seconds remaining in our session. A thought floated through my mind. Maybe Torres saw a hundred couples like Ralph and me every year and none of them made it. Maybe she already knew that it was hopeless. That I was seeking help when it was far too late to do so.

"I'm going to be straight with you."

I took a deep breath, focusing on the purple frames still sitting precariously near the end of her nose. I rubbed my hands together. I could get through anything. And if it was bad, I'd just hand over my cheque, scurry out to my car, and never come back.

She leaned forward and placed both hands flat on either side of her legal pad. "What you are doing is not working."

She used my silence to continue her point. "Trying to convince Ralph by talking *at* him is not making your marriage better. With that in mind, I'm going to suggest you try something different. Something radically different. Are you up for it?"

"I, I think so." My face flushed, but, finally, we were down to business.

"When you see Ralph, stop talking to him about everything that is wrong with your life together. That means you can't tell him how much you hate his hobbies or that he is failing miserably as a husband. Do you think you can do that?"

"I, I..." Could I do that? "Well, I don't know. I have these feelings. Strong feelings. What will I do with them if I can't tell Ralph?"

"Do you have a good friend you trust?"

I nodded.

5

"Good. You can tell that person. You can tell me. You can journal your frustrations. You can yell in the shower when Ralph is out larping. But for goodness' sake, you cannot keep telling Ralph. You have already told him. Likely several dozen times. It is not changing the situation, wouldn't you agree?"

"Well, now that you put it that way…yes. I agree. It's not changed the situation."

"I'm only asking that you try it. Until our next appointment. To create a cooling-off period."

"All right." I was nodding like a damn bobblehead stuck in a wind tunnel of confusion. This was it?

"Assignment number two," said Torres, "if you are looking for some bonus points." Surely she would have something, anything, productive for me to do. She had, after all, a billion years of education, if the letters after her name meant anything. "Keep your eyes open for spur-of-the-moment opportunities to inject a little goodwill into your relationship. It doesn't need to be big. Just everyday moments. It's about trying to remember that you – at some point – liked Ralph."

I was paying for this?

"Will you need a receipt for your benefit plan, Gillian?"

I apparently was.

Chapter Two

I was in a state of semi-disbelief, and the last person I wanted to see was Ralph. Well, second-last to Celeste Torres. I'd spilled my guts to someone who'd basically told me to stop hyperventilating. I ground my teeth. There may have been more to it than that, but I was still processing. So instead of going home, I drove to the yoga studio.

When it comes to ways of contemplating life's challenges, there are a lot of options. Some people look for answers at church. Others seem to find meaning through volunteerism or through long stretches of solitude surrounded by nature. For others, a bottle of wine works wonders. I don't discount the wine, but I have found yoga results in less hangover and tighter triceps.

I arrived at the studio and laid claim to my favourite spot directly under the cold-air return vent. The room could get exceedingly warm and I already felt overheated most days. This grim reminder of my aging was not only uncomfortable but also needless. The deepening creases on my forehead were doing a fine job of reminding me all on their own.

Unrolling my mat on the hardwood practice floor, I lay down and stretched first one hamstring, then the other. Participants were trickling in, each one busy setting out their mat, chatting to neighbours, or stretching as I was. Outwardly, I'm pretty sure I blended in: the perfectly calm, mindful yoga practitioner in black stretchy capris (yes, that is an anti-roll control top band, and yes, it's worth the extra money) and a purple tank top which, if I may say so, shows off my yoga-defined shoulders rather nicely. I'm particularly proud of them, and I swear it's all because of the yoga.

But inside was another story. My mind was racing like a manic rat rehashing the dreadful therapy session, one painful moment after another. What had Torres meant when she'd raised her eyebrows and asked for clarification? Or when she'd sniffed? Was that her way of showing disdain or did she have a runny nose?

When the yoga instructor entered and welcomed the class, it was a relief knowing I'd soon have something else to focus on. Using the hair elastic from around my wrist, I swept my wayward hair up into my signature bun. The haphazard knot on top of my head was certainly not a Hollywood-inspired French chignon, and yet it usually kept my hair out of my face and somewhat in control for the entirety of a class.

Before long, we'd begun the repetitive motions that were so familiar to me. The process was supposed to warm the body (a goal I was successfully achieving) and help clear the mind (um, clear failure). Today my agitation refused to be simply swept under the yoga mat.

I had a husband who would rather spend his weekends chasing other grown adults (forward bend) through the forest (plank) rather than spend time with me (upward dog). And I'd agreed to not complain about it (downward dog). To not say one damn thing about it (okay, still downward dog – what was with holding this pose for so long, anyway?).

Sure, every marriage had problems: shitty communication, laundry piled in the wrong spots, financial woes. That stuff was normal. But live-action role-play? Not normal. Why was it so hard for a therapist to understand that? A person, I might add, I was paying. Wasn't she supposed to take my side?

As I worked out multiple sun salutations, pretending to breathe as evenly as possible (although let's face it, no one breathes evenly while performing sun salutations, especially not when their hormones are squawking, *You, honey, are old. Let me send you a flash reminder in case you've forgotten*), my mind did what any mind might naturally do.

It did not enter some Zen state of nothingness. Nope. It slipped back in time to when the whole mess began.

"Pardon me?" I'd said. "Harping?"

"Lllarping," the flutist had corrected. "L-A-R-P. Live-action role-play, you know?" She'd answered my question with a smile but her predatory gaze had shifted to Ralph.

"Sorry," I said. "I don't know." We were at a gala fundraising dinner for the Philharmonic Orchestra. I'd been performing with them for several years. My instrument, the French horn, might not have been the sexiest, but it was solid. Substantial. Not some flighty, erratic-sounding woodwind reminiscent of a chickadee caught sucking helium.

I took a sip of my wine and wondered how we could politely exit this conversation. Lauren, a flutist who had recently joined the orchestra, was droning on about her gap year after university, while Ralph, more interested in his bacon-wrapped artichoke, had been zero help keeping the stilted discussion going. Zero help until she'd dropped larp on him like crack cocaine.

Ralph looked up from his plate. "Live action. Is that like acting out a scene from a game? In real time or something?"

Lauren nodded.

"Doesn't it attract some strange people?" he asked. His attention was already moving back to his appetiser. "You know, Dungeon & Dragons types who haven't left their basements since the 1970s?"

I gave a polite chuckle.

But not Lauren.

She howled.

She threw her head back, long blonde waves streaming over her bare shoulders, as though Ralph had said the funniest thing ever. The swell of her breasts nearly bounced over the deep neckline of her turquoise gown.

Brother.

I self-consciously smoothed my black dress – the same

9

one I'd worn to last year's event – over my Spanx, which were unfortunately cutting off circulation to my abdomen.

"Larp attracts all types," Lauren said, having managed to catch her breath before her breasts escaped clean out of her dress. "If you like adventure and the outdoors and excitement, you'll like this." She directed her response at Ralph, who had, after all, asked the question. "You should check out our website sometime. It lists all our upcoming events." Reaching into her purse, she pulled out a business card and handed it to Ralph.

"Oh, er, thanks." He balanced his plate in one hand, handing his wine glass to me while pocketing the business card.

I'd found it there later. I'd taken the card with its heavily embossed gold print out of his pocket before throwing his dress pants in the wash.

And if I hadn't found it? The card would've been mashed to a wet pulp and torn into several mucky pieces, later to clog the dryer vent with the rest of the lint. Would that have changed anything?

Perhaps not. We live in the Internet age. Yet I still couldn't help wondering.

Because instead of discarding it, I'd placed the larp card in the basket with loose pocket change and odd socks, the ones whose matches were forever MIA.

And there the card had sat. Waiting to be rediscovered.

And, of course, it had been. All it took was the right series of events. A crisis had hit – the unthinkable had happened. Then, incomprehensibly, life had moved on.

I had remodelled the kitchen.

Ralph had bought leather-studded armour.

I lay in corpse pose in the now-dim studio. The yoga class was ending and everyone around me was rolling up their mats. I must've missed the Namaste. I used the palm of my hand to wipe away the errant tear that had rolled down my temple and puddled in my hairline before I rolled up my own mat and left.

Sitting in my car, I thumbed out a quick text to Jas.

Up for a drink?

It was, after all, Friday night.
I didn't have to wait long for her reply.

Wish I could.   Have to help my mother with a few details before tomorrow.

Oh. Right. Mr Singh's eightieth birthday party.
A second text from Jas quickly followed the first.

You're coming, right?

Wouldn't miss it. Arianna bored? I could take her to a movie. Get her out for a while.

Arianna was Jas's fourteen-year-old daughter and an only child. She also happened to be the brightest, most lovely child I'd ever met as well as my and Ralph's goddaughter. Not only was Jas my best friend but she and Arianna were the closest thing we had to family in the city.

Darn. She's at a friend's. Working on a science project.

On a Friday night?

I was sceptical.

It's due next week.

What did I know, anyway? It wasn't as though I had a kid of my own in middle school. My phone beeped with another text from Jas.

So? Are you going to tell me how it went??

Jas had been supportive when I'd confided my scheduled appointment with Dr Torres. But other than her, I'd kept it to myself – had not even told Ralph. I thought for a minute before responding.

I'm still processing.

Oh? Can't wait to hear.

Hope you can handle the suspense until tomorrow!

Then I punched out a goodbye and put the phone away. Without any further distractions, I headed home.

Chapter Three

Glancing at my watch, I congratulated myself on successfully biting my tongue for twenty hours. And the next few hours should be a breeze; I couldn't think of one reason either Ralph or I would need to bring up larp while at a birthday party for an eighty-year-old man. Especially when most of the other guests would be speaking Punjabi.

As luck would have it, we were walking up to the Singhs' door just as Jas and Arianna drove up. We waited on the front walk until Jas found parking and joined us. Even from a distance I could see that Jas was wearing a traditional sari in bright emerald with a pink and orange trim. I was used to seeing her in fitted business suits or jeans and sweaters, and I knew without asking she was wearing traditional clothing to honour and please her parents. Her shoulder-length hair bounced with each step and the sun glinted off the gold bangles on her wrists. Other than the pinched expression between her carefully manicured eyebrows, she looked lovely.

"I'm so glad you could come." Jas kissed Ralph on the cheek before giving me a hug. "Dad will be happy to see you!"

"We'd assumed you'd already be here," Ralph said.

"Yes, so did I," Jas said. "Best laid plans..."

I turned towards my goddaughter, ready to wrap her in a hug. Unlike her mother, she was dressed in modern Western clothing. Skinny jeans – if there was a brand called *extreme skinny*, these had to be them – long feather earrings, purple nails, and a fitted top. "Arianna, you look—"

"Too old," Jas cut in.

"I was going to say *mature*." I made quick eye contact

with Jas, wondering what the argument had been about this time.

"Thank you, Auntie." Arianna's voice was carefully void of any emotion. Not acknowledging her mother, she pointedly turned to Ralph, who did manage to envelop her in a big hug.

"How's my favourite swimmer doing?" he asked, Arianna's extracurricular activity being one of their favourite topics. They led the way inside, discussing distances, time trials, and stroke count, Jas and me trailing behind.

As predicted, the house was brimming over with guests. The happy sounds of Punjabi music and the tantalizing aroma of Indian food surrounded us immediately. Mr Singh was sitting in his brown La-Z-Boy by the front window, a heavy afghan covering his legs. As we made our way over to greet him, I heard snippets of conversation in both Punjabi and English. Of course, I only understood the English: boasts about children's academic successes, debates over potential real estate deals, and arguments about the likelihood of Pakistan beating England in the upcoming world cricket match.

"Happy Birthday, Dad!" Jas kissed her father in the space between his cheerful orange turban and the top rim of his glasses. In all the time I'd known Mr Singh, he'd kept his trademark look of flowing cotton robes and pants – which happened to be the favoured garment of most of the male guests in attendance. What struck me today was how frail he looked. Last time I'd seen him, he'd been out gardening in the yard. Was he ill? I gave myself a shake. He was probably healthier than I was – no meat, no wine, no fast food. He was just getting older, same as the rest of us.

Mr Singh smiled and patted his daughter on the cheek. "It is a happy day. Eighty years young. And look, my beautiful granddaughter!" He reached behind Jas to squeeze Arianna's wrist and pull her into a hug. A frown crossed his face.

"My dear, you look...different." His gaze shifted from

Arianna's neatly threaded eyebrows to her lightly shadowed eyelids and glossy lips before settling on her recently acquired fringe.

Jas had often confided that growing up in a traditional eastern family within a western culture had been difficult. Particularly when it had come to grooming. She'd worn long sleeves year-round to hide arm hair. Suffering in silence, she'd never told her parents about the endless teasing.

"It's just lip gloss, Papa." Arianna looked at her mother nervously and, regardless of what had transpired between them this morning, her mother responded in solidarity.

"She's nearly fifteen, Dad. And she lives in Canada. She's Canadian. Lots of Sikh Canadian girls wear makeup."

I looked down and shuffled my feet, fumbling with the small wrapped gift I'd brought.

Ralph cleared his throat. "Not a lot of men your age have such beautiful admirers, that's for sure." He shook the older man's hand. "Happy Birthday, Mr Singh."

The frown that was wrinkling Mr Singh's forehead smoothed out and he nodded. "A beautiful young woman here to celebrate my birthday. I certainly am a blessed man."

Arianna smiled gratefully at Ralph and gave her grandfather a hug. "I'm going to say hello to Grandmother." Waving to the rest of us, she weaved her way through the crowded living room in the direction of the kitchen.

I breathed a sigh of relief. I hated tension. It'd been really tough when Jas had married Keith, a white Canadian who happened to be Ralph's friend. That was, in fact, how I'd met Jas in the first place. Jas's parents had wanted a more traditional marriage for their only daughter, and so their relationship with both Jas and Keith had been seriously strained. Until their granddaughter was born. She'd tied them all together and kept it that way.

"Happy Birthday, Mr Singh." Leaning over, I handed him the small gift I carried. He patted my hand with his own, a feather-light touch of thanks, and a grin spread across his features.

"Better hide those from Mom," Jas said, eyeing the rectangular box.

He and I both loved chocolate, but Mrs Singh refused to buy any on account of his cholesterol. "Life's small pleasures." I winked. "Besides, we'll probably eat you out of house and home today. Ralph didn't eat breakfast so he could save room for Mrs Singh's cooking." On cue, Ralph rubbed his tummy and we all laughed. Ralph loved food and was the kind of guy who could eat whatever he wanted without gaining weight.

Leaving Ralph to the buffet table and Mr Singh to a group of elderly men who had just arrived, Jas and I went to see if her mother needed any help with hosting duties. But on our way to the kitchen, Jas waylaid me into the hallway.

"Okay, so how'd it go?"

I didn't need to ask what she was referring to. I gave her the quick scoop, including my assigned homework. In the retelling, it sounded straight out of a self-help book one might find on the discount table at the bookstore. I shrugged. "That's about it."

"Let me get this straight. Your therapist wants you to stop talking to Ralph?"

"Actually, I think she wants me to stop talking," I paused to make air quotes for Jas's benefit, "'*at*' him. You know, about everything that's wrong. I can talk about anything else as long as I avoid, well, the usual subjects."

Jas's eyebrows shot up. "But…correct me if I'm wrong…is there anything else to talk about?"

"Good Lord, who knows?"

"Did she suggest anything else?"

"I'm supposed to," again I used the air quotes, "'*inject some goodwill*'. I'm basically supposed to be nice. And try to remember I like him." I grimaced. It sounded horribly mean coming out of my mouth. Did I not like my husband? Down the hallway, I could see him chatting with a stranger. He looked relaxed, his auburn hair a bit ruffled from the wind outside, as he listened to what the stranger was saying.

16

I'd always loved how intently he listened. I missed how he used to listen to me like that. How had we become so disconnected? I turned away.

"Honestly, Jas, I don't have any better ideas. I might as well give it a go." It surely couldn't make things worse than our current roommate-I-can-barely-tolerate situation.

Jas gave my arm a squeeze. "It can't hurt. Too much!"

We laughed and continued into the kitchen.

Jas's mother, Mrs Singh, was surrounded by several other women in the equally crowded kitchen. Every available surface was covered in chafing dishes filled with vegetarian curries, delicious lentil entrees, and Indian sweet pudding.

"How many people are you expecting, Momma?" Jas hugged her tiny mother about the shoulders. Mrs Singh, who wasn't quite five feet tall, could produce an extraordinary amount of energy. Her hair, swept back in a tight bun, was threaded with more silver than black, and her petite body was draped in a sari the colour of sunshine.

"Everyone we love," she said.

"So...too many."

"Oh, Jaspreet, you know I love to cook, and I love hosting people."

"But do you love the cleanup?" I said. Mrs Singh stood on tiptoe to kiss my cheek in welcome.

"It is no trouble."

I looked over her head and shared a smile with Jas. We would've been surprised if her answer had been anything different.

"Can I help carry some of this food out?" I waved in the general direction of the warming dishes. Most guests would be helping themselves to food from the buffet set up in the dining room, and everything in here was used to keep those dishes full.

"Of course not, dear. You two should eat. Go!" She shooed us out, smiling. "Enjoy yourselves."

Leaving the kitchen, we made our way to the family dining room. The table, pushed against one wall, was covered by several Indian delicacies. As Jas continued to mingle with her parents' guests, collecting used plates and cutlery as she went, I heaped my plate with spiced lentils, aromatic curries, and my favourite vegetable paneer.

Okay, where to now? I knew, like, practically no one.

Thank goodness it was easy to spot Ralph, his being one of the only Caucasian faces in the crowded room. He was in the far corner of the living room, chatting with a man I didn't recognise. Heading over in my husband's direction, I regretted filling my plate as full as I had; it was a veritable minefield between the rice sauces on my plate, the beautiful saris of the guests, and the Singh's white carpet.

I smiled with relief when I joined them disaster-free. Now I only had to figure out how to stand, converse, and eat without spilling all over myself – easy, right? I nodded in greeting at the man Ralph was talking with. A head taller than Ralph, his frame was lean and he wore a traditional turban with western-style clothing.

They continued their conversation on NHL first-round draft picks, and I didn't even bother pretending interest. The food, as always, was ridiculously delicious. I savoured every bite, pushing aside thoughts of heavy cream and rich butter before using my last piece of naan to scoop up as much of the remaining sauce as I could. Nothing this tasty should be wasted.

Out of the crowd, Mrs Singh appeared, pulling a somewhat reluctant Jas behind her.

"Mrs Singh, the food is delicious," said Ralph in greeting. The other man and I heartily agreed.

"There is plenty of food, please help yourselves to more," said Mrs Singh with a beaming smile. "Mr Chawla, I see you have met our friends. I would also like to introduce you to my daughter, Jaspreet Singh-Barber." I couldn't help but smile as I looked from Mrs Singh, with her face wreathed in happy creases, to Jas with her frozen features.

Mrs Singh leaned in to Mr Chawla. "Jaspreet is a veeery accomplished lawyer. Specialised in environmental protection! I think you have a lot in common."

A slow flush crossed Jas's cheekbones. I took a sip of water to hide my smile.

With a quick push, Mrs Singh positioned Jas in front of Mr Chawla. She then turned to Ralph. "Go. Eat more!" she instructed before floating back to the kitchen.

Wow. I tried hard to smother a laugh, but jeez, it wasn't easy. The silence was lengthening into the realm of uncomfortable, and I shot a glance at Ralph. He shrugged his shoulders and headed back to the buffet. No help there.

"Oh, I'm sorry. I didn't catch your first name?" I reached my hand out towards the tall stranger.

"Bendar." He shook my hand and returned my smile.

"Nice to meet you, Bendar. I'm Ralph's wife, Gillian. We're friends with Jas. Jaspreet." I looked over at Jas, but she still didn't seem prepared to join the conversation. All right, carry on I would.

"Have you been in Calgary long?"

"Only about six weeks. I'm from Vancouver and just came out on a contract. My family is pretty much all on the West Coast."

"That must be lonely," said Jas. I looked over, surprised at her sudden contribution. "Will your wife and children be joining you here?" A brittle smile spread across her face.

"I was actually referring to my parents. And sisters. I have nieces and a nephew there too." He took his phone out from his inside jacket pocket and began flipping through photos. "See, I'm worse than an old grannie." He held the phone out for me. Three pudgy and healthy-looking Indian preschool children smiled back at me. The leafy trees and sea wall in the distance indicated the photo was likely taken at Stanley Park. "It's hardest to be away from them. Cute little buggers." He raised an eyebrow and added, "Not so hard to be away from my sisters, though, if you know what I mean."

As he smiled, happy little wrinkles around his eyes betrayed him for someone who made it a practice to be happy. I smiled back. He was certainly attractive. But my friend seemed to be immune to Bendar's charm.

19

"I'm sure I don't know what you mean." Her voice was like a bucket of ice on the conversation. What the heck? Couldn't she see the little lines?

"My sisters, you see, feel it is their personal mission to find me a wife. They are forever setting me up with people they have pre-screened, so to speak."

Caught off guard, Jas laughed. "Oh, I see. Yes, no one needs that. It's a little, um, presumptuous at times, isn't it?" Finally, my friend was letting her guard down. They had found common ground despite her determination not to.

"Yes, it is." He put his phone away, the little wrinkles by his eyes disappearing as he stared at Jas pointedly. Looked like he wasn't interested in Mrs Singh's set-up either.

I glanced at Jas, biting my lip.

She cleared her throat. "Have you seen Arianna?"

I took her lead, knowing it was my duty to help her out of the awkward situation. "Not since arriving. Perhaps we should look for her?" I smiled at Bendar. "Excuse us."

"What the hell?" I whispered as soon as we were out of earshot.

"I know. Sorry." Jas walked briskly, a no-nonsense smile on her face. We gathered used plates and glasses as we wound our way through the crowd. "Can you believe my mother tried to set me up?"

"Are you sure that's what she was doing?"

Jas gave me an incredulous look, her cheeks flushed with annoyance. "Of course she was. Why else the 'you have so much in common' line. Jeez! I'm forty-freaking-five." Although true, Jas could pass for at least ten years younger. Her hair was still jet black, not a single strand of grey woven through it.

"I don't think you'll need to worry about him," I said in as soothing a voice as I could manage. Regardless of how young she looked, my friend was one of those vicious dogs that looked cute and fluffy on the outside, but if you stretched your hand out to pet it – *snap*! "What, ah, turned you off in the first place?"

We handed off the dirty dishes to a group of elderly

women in the kitchen who were speaking rapid-fire Punjabi. I smiled and nodded in what I considered a very respectful fashion.

"Seems traditional. I'm not cooking and cleaning for some man."

"Right. He was probably already picturing you in an apron."

"Funny. Well, he's certainly not interested in any case." A quick scan of the kitchen told us Arianna was not there. "Let's check upstairs. She'd better not be in some dark corner texting her friends. I'm starting to regret buying her that thing."

We made our way up the stairs. All of the doors leading off the hallway were closed, and the only light was seeping out from under the bathroom door.

Jas pounded on the door. "Arianna."

An elderly man's voice responded. "One minute, please."

"Oh! Sorry, Mr Punni. Take your time." Jas backed away from the door and gave me a sheepish look.

"Maybe the basement?" I suggested. "Or the backyard?"

"Let's try the bedrooms first," whispered Jas out of respect for Mr Punni. "This is the room she uses when she sleeps over." Jas indicated a door on her left. Opening it, she reached in and switched the light on before peeking her head inside.

"Mother!" My goddaughter's voice, shrill with righteous indignation and surprise, pierced my eardrum.

"Arianna!"

I looked over Jas's shoulder just in time to see a young man jumping up from the single bed.

"I'm sorry! I'm sorry! Nothing happened!" His voice broke in midstream. He managed to duck past me and race downstairs – practically colliding with a flustered Mr Punni, who had been attempting to make a discreet exit from the bathroom – before I could get a good look at his face.

I covered my mouth to keep from laughing. Fifteen wasn't young by today's standards. I'd asked Jas a few

21

times if Arianna was dating anyone. But Jas had always given me the same answer – Arianna wasn't interested in boys – which I highly doubted. We'd all been her age once upon a time. But now was hardly the time to say *told you so*.

Arianna stood up and straightened her shirt. A look of righteous indignation was on her face, and I didn't need to see Jas's to know the same look would be mirrored. Maybe I could help break the ice before tempers got the best of them?

"So…seems like a…good-looking young man. Who is he?" My voice sounded overly cheerful, even to me.

Arianna shrugged. "Just some guy."

"Just some guy?" said Jas. "Are you kidding me? You're making out with a random *just some guy* at your grandparents' house?"

Shit. Maybe that had been a bad question to begin with.

"Perhaps I'll just go downstairs…" I started.

"No, Auntie. It's fine," said Arianna.

I glanced at Jas, but she was completely focused on her daughter. She walked into the room, sat down on the edge of the bed, and folded her hands in her lap. She took a few deep breaths before speaking.

"I don't think I've met him before, have I?"

Arianna rolled her eyes. "If you ever came to the gurdwara, you would have."

Arianna attended the Sikh temple with her grandparents when she slept over at their place, but I knew Jas rarely attended.

Jas didn't respond to the barbed statement or the defiant glare and instead let both slip by. "Are you dating? Do his parents know?"

"Mom! Do his parents know what? Of course we aren't dating! It's nothing. I definitely don't think he would've told his parents when nothing's going on. And I definitely," Arianna pointed her finger at her mother, "don't think they would be spying on their son."

"I wasn't spying! Just checking. I trust you, and I know

you will make good decisions."

I wondered why conversations with teenaged kids got antagonistic so quickly. I suppose I'd been the same way with my own mother, but I couldn't help feeling overwhelmed by the situation unfolding in front of me. For once, I was glad it wasn't me who was the parent.

Jas smiled in a somewhat wooden way and tried once again. "I can understand you are curious and it's all very exciting. That's okay, as long as you are safe."

Oh dear. Arianna had turned to solid rock.

"I always keep, you know, extra condoms in my purse," I blurted. "Help yourself, anytime." Unfortunately, no one thought it was funny but me. "Ha ha. Kidding, of course." I hated tension. I wished I could help Arianna out of this awkward situation, and I wished I could help Jas manoeuvre it into a safe zone, but I was at a loss how to help either one of them.

"Arianna, honey," Jas continued as though I hadn't interrupted. "You are smart and strong, and you do not need a boy. You know that, right?"

This was going to turn into a disaster, that was easy to see, whether I was here or not. "I think I'll just go downstairs and see if your grandma needs any help in the kitchen."

I started backing out of the room but Arianna held up her hand to stop me. "It's okay, I'll check on her." As she spoke her pissed-right-off gaze did not leave her mother's face. "That's right, Mom. Because I want to be all alone, like you. Gee, that seems like a lot of fun." Arianna gave me a last wooden smile before storming out of the room.

After her departure, I closed the door gently, allowing Jas a few minutes to compose herself. She hadn't moved, and so I sat down beside her on the bed, letting her be the first to speak.

"Guess she wasn't texting."

I smiled. "Guess you're right."

"I botched that."

"You did fine." I put my arm around her. "I think

23

everyone was surprised."

"Did you see that kid's face?" Jas said.

"I saw extremely large eyes before he peed his pants and took off."

Jas laughed. We sat in silence for a bit, and I didn't press her for her thoughts.

"I'm going to have to let go a bit."

"Yup."

"It was just, you know, I wasn't ready for it."

"She's a smart girl." I said. "Fifteen soon."

"But she's going to make mistakes."

"We all did."

Jas leaned her head on my shoulder and I patted her knee. "This sucks."

"It does." I agreed. "Wine would help."

"Believe me, as soon as I get home." Jas's parents didn't drink, so there was no hope of finding any around here. We listened to the cheerful sounds filtering up the stairs from the party for several minutes before Jas voiced what was probably most on her mind. "I wonder what Keith would say."

My heart skipped a beat. It always did when his name came up. I wasn't good with grief, and I rarely said the right thing. As usual, I scrambled to fill the silence.

"He'd say you're doing a good job."

"Do you think Arianna's right? My life's boring?"

"It's not boring. It's busy…with everyone else."

"What am I supposed to do? My parents are old. My daughter's young."

"I know. Sandwich generation." I didn't know, of course. Not from experience anyway. But I'd heard about it from a lot of people my age. "You're doing a great job, Jas. It's just – are you lonely? Not that marriage is necessarily much better," we both knew I was referring to my own, "but do you ever think of dating?"

Jas shrugged. "I think, after all these years on my own, I've become some bitter old hag."

I smiled. "At the age of forty-five? Probably."

24

"It's hard to find someone."

"Especially when you aren't looking."

"Where am I supposed to look? The gym? The bar? Have my parents arrange something for me? No thanks!"

"Maybe at work?"

"Ha. Sounds fun and not at all complicated." But there was a smile back in her voice. "Am I too picky?"

"Yup."

Jas smiled and stood up from the bed. She took one last look around the room. Everything seemed to be in its place.

"Good thing Papa didn't find them in here. He'd have had a heart attack!"

I stood up and we exited the room. "Small miracles. All around us, I suppose."

Chapter Four

"You should've seen the look on that kid's face," I said after giving Ralph a rundown of the dramatic events that had occurred in the Singhs' guest room. We were driving home in the twilight hours, the sun slowly setting behind the distant mountains that skirted our city. "I don't know where Arianna's young Romeo escaped to, but we didn't see him the rest of the evening."

Ralph laughed. "That's got to be every fifteen-year-old's worst nightmare: getting caught by the parents. I remember those days fondly myself." He reached over the central console of the Camry and squeezed my knee.

Without consciously thinking about it, I drew my leg away. Ralph put his hand back on the steering wheel.

Damn. I was pretty certain how Dr Torres might analyse my behaviour. Even I could admit it fell squarely within the *What you're doing isn't working* category and certainly not the *Building goodwill* category.

"It, ah, appears Jas is not into the whole dating scene," I said, attempting to fill the dead air between us. "Whether it's Arianna or herself."

"True," agreed Ralph. "What was her problem with that Bendar guy? He seemed nice enough to me."

Thinking back over our conversation, I pictured Jas's rigid jaw line and antagonistic body language. "I think she resented that her mother was trying to set her up. And she was trying to make it clear to him that she does not need a man."

Ralph laughed again, but this time it seemed to have a bitter edge. "Who does?"

I crossed my arms. "Maybe she's not ready."

The car filled with our usual silence. I contemplated time, and how much a person might need before they were ready for something new. How months and even years could pass while some people's lives stood still and others' moved forward as though nothing significant had happened. Then there were those who got busy doing useless things like prancing through the woods in pretend armour.

I snuck a peek at Ralph. He was focused on the road. Who was he to cast the first stone, anyway? Normally I might say something, but I remembered my homework assignment. Instead, I looked out my window and watched the suburban streets fly by in the dimming light.

Ralph turned on the radio and began flipping through stations. He settled on hockey game commentary. Shit. Following Dr Torres's supposed wisdom was torture. I had limits.

I looked over at Ralph. "Really?" He knew I hated sports commentary.

"What?" He tapped the steering wheel in agitation. "It's playoffs."

I fished my phone out of my purse and started scrolling through Facebook updates in an attempt to block out the testosterone-infused play-by-play. Playoffs. Right.

Five minutes later, Ralph pulled up in front of our place and turned the engine off. "By the way, I invited Bendar to join us on Wednesday. You can get three tickets, right?"

I looked up from collecting my purse and undoing my seatbelt. "Bendar? From the party?"

Ralph nodded.

"Jas is going to be annoyed." One of the perks of my job with the Philharmonic was access to free tickets. With a new performance just starting, both Ralph and Jas had been planning to attend this week.

"Well, that's silly. He's new to town. He doesn't know anyone. I thought it would be nice."

I grimaced. "Sure, it's nice of you. But good luck if Jas thinks it's a set-up."

Ralph shrugged his shoulders as though it were no big

deal. Was I married to a complete emotional colander? I managed to swallow down my irritation. It would, after all, be his problem, not mine. I'd be the one safely on stage doing my job, and it'd be him responsible for mitigating an awkward situation.

We got out of the car and headed inside. I retired to the bedroom and my book, Ralph to the television room and his hockey game.

I woke up the next morning and rolled over. Ralph was snoring peacefully. His face was relaxed and his legs were spread eagle, taking up most of the bed. Obviously, he was enjoying his Sunday morning sleep in.

I quietly got up and dressed without disturbing him. I made it a regular habit of spending Sunday mornings in a restorative yoga class with Jas. Between her employment, her role as single mother, her commitment to helping her aging parents, and my, well, somewhat flexible work hours, the Sunday morning yoga class was something we held sacred.

I wouldn't be long, maybe two hours, and Ralph would just be rolling out of bed when I got back. I frowned. Unless he had one of those larp meetings? I couldn't remember.

After eating a light breakfast of granola, berries, and yogurt, I drove to the studio, parked, and scooted into the building with ten minutes to spare. Water trickled in the slate fountain and spicy sandalwood incense warmed the air. The studio's Zen atmosphere immediately affected me. Breathing the calm energy into my lungs, I was glad I'd made the effort to get up and go to class.

Jas arrived a few minutes after and we set up our mats, spending the few minutes before class stretching and chatting about the night before and the week ahead. It wasn't long before the instructor closed the practice room doors and welcomed everyone. This signalled the class was about to begin. After a series of sun salutations that resulted in heating up the class, fogging the windows, and creating a trickle of sweat between my shoulder blades, I was more

28

than ready for the second part of the class, which usually involved more stretching and less exertion. But the instructor had another idea.

"Today I'd like to try doing our floor work in pairs." She smiled at us from the front of the class, where she sat in lotus position with apparent ease. "Please find a partner and grab a cloth strap from the props cupboard. We'll be using the straps to assist our partners in deepening their stretches, thereby helping to release pressure on the spine."

Although we'd occasionally done partner work in the past, it didn't happen frequently. I turned to Jas. "Your mat?" I asked.

"Sure. I'll grab a strap." Jas stood up, took three steps off her mat, and bumped headfirst into a male participant.

At the look on Jas's face, I put my hand to my mouth and tried to stifle a nervous laugh. It turned into a funny coughing sound.

"Excuse me," said the stranger. He reached his hand out and steadied Jas by holding her shoulder. "Are you okay?"

Jas's cheeks were pink with exertion – and perhaps embarrassment. She tilted her head up to look at the man speaking, and I followed her gaze.

The stranger had close-cropped hair, startling blue eyes, and a jaw that looked straight off a Gillette commercial. He looked like the kind of person who lived outdoors and only drank protein shakes for dinner.

"Oh! Yes, I'm fine," stammered Jas. "I was just headed over to pick up a strap." She pointed towards the milling circle of participants waiting in line at the props cupboard, all trying to gather the required cloth strap. "Sorry, I didn't mean to plough you over."

"No worries. I never mind a good ploughing." The stranger grinned and Jas's jaw dropped. I suddenly felt like I was eavesdropping on a private conversation.

I lowered my eyes, which resulted in an unplanned check-out of the guy's forearms, when he asked Jas if she would like to partner.

Jas looked over at me and started motioning in my

direction. "Ah…" That was all she seemed to be able to vocalise.

I raised my eyebrows. With hyper-speed, my thoughts raced back to our conversation in the Singhs' spare bedroom. Where to meet someone, indeed? I flashed a friendly smile. "Oh, I'm actually partnering with…"

I looked around the room. There had to be someone; there always was. An older woman in hot pink was standing alone in the centre of the room, clenching a strap in her hands. She looked terrified of being the last picked. We made eye contact, and when I motioned for her to come over, her face flooded with relief.

"Her." I grinned at Jas and the chiselled protein drinker. "Have fun!" Jas gave me the stink eye before following the stranger to his mat. "Don't forget a strap," I called in farewell.

It turned out my partner and I got on quite comfortably. Our first pose involved one person resting in child's pose while the other pressed firmly down on their hips. This was done by straddling over them and applying counter pressure to their lower back.

"Remember," said the instructor, "it's a gentle pressure, only enough to allow the tension in your partner's lower back to release and their tailbone to sink towards the floor. Don't forget your *ujjayi* breath. And please communicate with your partner if the pressure is too great or too subtle."

As I carefully applied pressure to my partner's back, I glanced at my friend, but I couldn't see much. She was curled up in child's pose with the handsome stranger straddling her backside, her waist grasped firmly in his hands.

Dear Lord. I swallowed a nervous giggle. I didn't need to see Jas's face to guess what she might be thinking.

"And the second pose," continued the instructor after some minutes had passed, "requires the strap." She directed a volunteer to move into downward dog. This essentially meant creating an inverted *V* with your body: your hands and feet on the ground with your bottom in the air. "Place the strap under your partner's waist and apply counter pressure." The instructor held both ends of the strap firmly in her hands and pulled the volunteer's hips slightly in her direction. "Make sure to stand right between your partner's legs, one foot in front of the other, so as not to lose your balance. And again, remember to communicate. Your partner won't get any benefit if you don't apply firm pressure, but it shouldn't be uncomfortable either."

As my partner moved into downward dog, Jas looked over at me with equal parts dread and shock. She gave her tank top a good tug up and over her well-endowed chest before getting into position with chiselled protein drinker standing between her legs.

After what seemed an inordinately long time, we ended the class with corpse pose and a collective Namaste. I could hardly wait to get outside where Jas and I could safely rehash the situation.

"Do you know how hard it is to suck in your gut when doing a downward dog? My fat arse must've been in his face." My friend looked shaken but also intensely pleased.

"He didn't seem to mind. How about the first pose? The one where his hands were on your hips?"

"You mean when my middle-aged thighs pressed against his backside, or the other way around? 'Cause honestly, my vag hasn't been that close to a man – excluding my doctor – in years. To think, my greatest intimacy in nearly a decade occurred in yoga with a complete stranger."

I laughed. Jas laughed. It had been an unpredictable morning.

Jas rubbed her hands on her hips. "Jeez, I should do something about these."

"You're a woman, not a toothpick."

"Right. I'll remind Daniel if he comments."

"Daniel?"

Jas bobbed her head. "Yup. That's his name." Her cheeks flushed and she looked like the most beautiful person I'd ever seen.

She was happy

Chapter Five

Driving home in the midmorning sun, I played my music louder than usual and drummed along on my steering wheel. I was delighted for Jas. I hadn't seen her interested in anything male in eons.

I tried to ignore the other thing it had done, which was to shine a light on the shortcomings in my own marriage. But once the seed was planted in my consciousness, it was hard to ignore. Even if I didn't admit it to anyone, I'd long ago decided that marriage involved trading in excitement and passion for stability and comfort. Wasn't that what inevitably happened to all relationships once the years slipped by? I wondered, and not for the first time, if the trade was possibly not worth it.

New attraction seemed like a pair of shiny stiletto heels you couldn't wait to wear. When you pulled them out of the box and put them on, they might pinch your heel, but they had the strange power to make your ankles look slimmer and your legs appear longer.

But marriage was more like that old pair of hiking boots in the back of your closet. You could walk for miles and not get blisters. But they were scuffed with life's disappointments, brutal disagreements, and hard feelings. Compared to the stilettos, the hikers might be sturdy, but they looked entirely shabby and left you feeling anything but sexy.

I wasn't interested in Daniel myself. What I missed was being noticed. I missed someone being interested in me. And I missed the feeling that came with wearing those brand new shiny stilettos.

I pulled up in front of the renovated two-storey colonial

we called home and parked behind Ralph's car. I was a bit surprised to see it. Maybe he didn't have a larp gathering today after all?

This could be an opportunity. The type my therapist had suggested looking for: a moment to inject a little goodwill into my relationship with Ralph. Perhaps Torres was right. Perhaps my marriage would improve if I only tried something different. Perhaps it was my responsibility to kick off the old hiking boots and try something new. I could, at the least, try.

I smiled at the visual that popped into my head, took a deep breath, puffed out my chest, and slammed my car door shut before marching up to my own front door. I was doing this. I, Gillian Campbell, could do this. I thrust open the front door and kicked off my proverbial hiking boots.

"Rise and shine, Ralph!" I practically sang in greeting. "Let's go for brunch! And a walk! Why not? It's absolutely beautiful out."

I heard Ralph pounding up the stairs before I saw him. The ominous sound of cheap metal accompanied him. My heart sank.

Sure enough, Ralph rounded the corner, carrying an armload of larp battle gear: a flipping chest plate, leather-studded belt, helmet, and other bullshit odds and ends I wasn't familiar with.

"I'm so glad you're home, Gillian. My car's busted. Damn alternator, I think. I need your car. I'm already late and my group is counting on me."

"Pardon me?"

"I'm late."

I dropped my rolled-up yoga mat on the tile floor. It landed with a slap. "Pardon me: the car is busted? And you want to take mine, thereby leaving me stranded for the day because you are worried about letting down your dress-up friends?"

Before I knew it, thoughts of infusing goodwill and sexy footwear were gone. Instead, we were instantly entrenched in our familiar battle positions. But unlike larp, this battle wasn't pretend. And it wasn't fun either.

Ralph was the first to break the silent standoff. "Do you think I'm not stressed already? I'll see about getting the car fixed on Monday. But I made a commitment, and you know I look forward to larp all week." Ralph ran his free hand through his hair. "I don't know why you do this. It's not like I make you feel guilty about your yoga."

Blood pulsed through my veins. In some part of my brain, I was vaguely amazed my body could go from zero adrenaline to all-out fury in less than thirty seconds. A few moments ago I'd actually been looking forward to a surprise date with my husband, but now I was wondering what the point in trying was. Obviously, I was the old shoe and larp was Ralph's version of a stiletto.

"Go." I held out my car keys. "Just go."

For the briefest moment, his fingertips touched my palm as he scooped up the proffered keys. I dropped my empty hand to my side.

"I'm sorry, Gill, I really am. I'll come home as soon as I'm done. I'll be back for dinner." He circled around me and left through the still-open doorway.

I listened to his footsteps heading down the walkway, knowing there was still time. Time to do this differently. I could run out, tell Ralph to have a good time. Instead, I sat down on the stairs and listened to him shove the jangling collection of dress-up armour into the trunk, start the engine and drive away.

I sat for a time on the stairs, surrounded by my empty house, before I gritted my teeth and got on with it. I had homework to do. I'd made a commitment, and I would see it through. At least until my next appointment with Torres.

Chapter Six

I spent the day in the kitchen. Seeing as I didn't have a car, I had to make dinner with the ingredients I had on hand. This turned out to be lasagne, my creative energies fuelled in large measure by righteous indignation and the impassioned vocals of Serena Ryder at a rather loud volume.

And perhaps a sip or two of Malbec.

I was practically through a bottle by the time Ralph returned.

"Sorry I'm a bit late," he called out from the entrance. "That new boffer I ordered finally arrived."

I took a sip of my wine. "That's a weapon, right?"

"You got it." Ralph came into the kitchen carrying a long sword. The muted grey blade was a few feet long, the hilt wrapped in a black leather binding. "In the world of larp, this is a great investment. Pricey, sure – nearly three hundred dollars – but practically indestructible against lesser swords, goblin weapons, magic…you name it, this weapon beats it."

I gritted my teeth. "You know, Ralph, when I suggested you get a hobby, I meant gardening, or playing baseball, or even lawn bowling. I did not mean spending all your time and money running through the forest with sponge knives." I laughed, trying to make my statement sound more like a joke.

Silence played on the energy currents as we faced off over the kitchen island. I did not for one minute believe his boffer could out power a pissed-off wife.

"It's a foam replica great sword. Circa 1470." His voice was calm, and it took me a moment to process his words.

"Pardon?"

"It's not a knife."

A frozen chill shot up my throat, and, as often happened, I responded more quickly than my brain could think. My hand slammed down on the cold granite countertop as the words exploded out of me. "Three hundred bucks and it's not even a real goddamn knife. Crazy, isn't it?" I could feel a ghastly smile stretch across my face as I sucked in air.

Come on, Gill. Calm down. It's not as if we were struggling to pay our bills. We lived a comfortable life, with zero dependants to worry about. I slowly counted to ten in my mind. This definitely wasn't going the right way. I gently picked up my half-empty wine glass and took a sip. "Dinner's ready."

Turning my back on the discussion, I opened the oven and removed the lasagne. Although it was ready an hour ago, I'd left it there to keep it warm.

"Sorry," I mumbled. "I'm just... I don't know. Tired, I guess."

"Okay. Sorry I was late. I'll just go change."

Ralph left the kitchen and I rolled my shoulders, trying to release tension in my upper back. This homework of Torres's was harder to do than I'd anticipated.

By the time Ralph returned to the kitchen, I had our plates set with a healthy serving of homemade lasagne – covered in melted Romano and mozzarella cheeses and browned to perfection – along with fresh salad and crispy garlic bread. Two glasses of wine sat at the ready, a new bottle of Malbec between them.

I took my first bite, the mix of pasta, cheese, beef, and tomatoes both comforting and delicious.

"Could you pass the salt, please?"

I swallowed. "There isn't salt on the table to pass, dear."

Ralph looked up from his plate and surveyed the table. "Oh. Hadn't realised. I'll go get it."

Pushing his chair back from the table, he made his way to the cabinet where we kept spices and dry baking ingredients.

"Where's the salt?"

I rolled my eyes. He couldn't see me anyway, so what did it hurt? "Right-hand side. Where it always is."

"Oh, yes. Here it is. Do you want me to grab pepper or anything?"

I took a deep breath and worked hard to respond in a neutral tone. I was using up my benefit plan for counselling, I reminded myself – benefits that might be better used for massage – but it was too late to get my money back. I might as well at least attempt to stick to the homework.

"No, thank you, Ralph. I added spices while simmering the meat sauce for an hour. Then I combined all the other ingredients in careful layers before baking it. It took about two hours. But I also managed to get all the laundry done."

Oops. Oh well, I'd at least been successful at keeping my tone pleasant. That must deserve a small reward. I took a sip of Malbec. What the heck, I took another before setting my glass back down with a clink.

Ralph returned to the table and gave his lasagne a healthy dose of heart-killing sodium.

"It's delicious, Gillian. Just needs a little salt."

Silence seemed a safe answer. Or maybe a change in topic might be in order.

"Any plans for this week?"

"Funny you should ask. I actually had an unusual idea today, and I think I might spend some time doing a little research."

I was scared to ask what his idea of unusual was, this coming from a man who larped, but I threw caution to the wind and did anyway. You know what they say – alcohol affects your judgement first before anything else.

"What's your idea?"

"It was kind of sparked by the whole process of getting this great sword. I asked Rick over two months ago if he'd mind picking it up for me when on his trip out east. He and his wife take an annual road trip with their motorhome."

"Motorhome trip?" I perked up. We'd done a fair amount of camping when we were younger, but never the motorhome kind. We'd been the kind of people who hiked in and out of the backcountry and carried everything on our backs. "That sounds interesting."

"Sure. They love it, I guess. But I'd hate cleaning out the plumbing system. Black water, grey water, who knows what you're supposed to do?" Ralph took a sip of his wine, and I put the holiday idea aside. I'd probably kill him anyway. I could picture us on some abandoned road, out of gas and stuck. Alone for possibly weeks on end.

"The thing is the boffer," said Ralph. "I had this business idea."

This took me by surprise. Ralph had been employed by the same company since we'd moved to Calgary and had never shown the slightest interest in leaving.

"That sounds…interesting." *Good job, Gill.* I gave myself a mental pat on the back for being supportive and dished myself out another serving of salad. "What, um, kind of business idea?" Yes, I was on a supportive roll. We were sustaining a conversation.

"The more I think about it, the more I'm convinced it could work. I'm thinking about starting up an online business. We've got some money saved, and I could use it as start-up capital for purchasing stock. Of course, I'll carefully research the items that are in highest demand." He was leaning forward in his excitement, his words coming out so fast they were practically stumbling on themselves.

Oh God. Being supportive was a bad idea. An online business? My husband had never been in sales, had never even worked for himself before. I doubted he knew the first thing about being an entrepreneur. How long had he been thinking about this?

"And, ah, what exactly are you thinking about selling through this online business?" I gave up on the salad and took a nip of wine to fortify myself.

"Gill, aren't you following? Live-action weapons. Maybe some costume items, but mainly weaponry. There's a huge market in town. And no real competition. The only local supplier focuses on costumes, and the boffers they keep stocked are extremely basic." Ralph's face was rapturous. He gulped his lasagne, chewing and swallowing quickly so he could continue with his train of thought. "Obviously I'll set up a website, use PayPal and money transfers. It'll be easy. I'll run a whole twitter campaign and have my own Facebook page. I have a lot of connections through live action, and I know I can really make a go of this. It's only a matter of using some of our savings as capital. To purchase the initial stock."

Our savings? I'd assumed that was for retirement. Or our annual beach holiday. Even a goddamn motorhome would be something I'd agree to. But this? Obviously plans changed sometimes. I just hadn't realised how much. My teeth ground my salad to a liquid as I listened to the insanity, and I could barely swallow.

"It's completely different from engineering. And you know, Gillian, I think that's what I need."

What the hell was this? "You're seriously thinking about giving up your day job?" I finally managed to get out.

"Not right away." Ralph ran a hand through his thinning hair. "But the global economy is less willing to invest in oil sands. I think it's as good a time as any to change it up." He stopped dreaming long enough to pour himself another glass of wine, thereby finishing the bottle.

I looked around at our middle-class – but certainly comfortable – dining room. I took in the wall art, hardwood floors, faux-rock fireplace, and triple-pane windows. The things I used to find comfort in seemed cold somehow. Meaningless.

Was my husband completely insane? Had he fallen and damaged his brain while cavorting in the park this afternoon?

"Are. You. In. Sane?" I said, stretching out the syllables so as not to be misunderstood. I put my fork down and clenched my hands together on my lap. "You want to put all our savings into a fucking mail-order costume shop? Are you on meth? Crack? Maybe Special fucking K?"

Silence.

It was some time before Ralph responded. "You never

support me, Gillian."

"That's not true!" I'd given up speaking in a neutral tone. This was too much.

Ralph folded his napkin in a precise, sharp-cornered square – once, twice, three times – then placed it on top of what was left of his salt and lasagne. He quietly said, "I supported your decision to go into the arts."

"That was almost twenty years ago! We didn't have a mortgage. We didn't have kids!"

"And we don't have kids now."

My heart froze. Of course we didn't have kids. Life was moving along, and I was standing still. Childless. Alone with a husband I couldn't speak to for the course of a meal without combusting into a fiery argument. A husband I couldn't understand and wasn't even friends with anymore.

I could tell by the way Ralph rubbed his temple that he already regretted mentioning the unmentionable. But it was too late to take it back. "It was just an idea," he mumbled. He got up, pushed in his chair with care, and walked away from the table.

I sat in silence until what was left of the evening light filtering in through the triple-paned glass dimmed and left me in darkness.

Ralph

Gillian sat frozen at the dining room table. She was staring out the window at God knows what. With her carefree hair subdued in a bun and her freckles constellations against her pale skin, she looked the fabled Ice Queen incarnate. It seemed a wise idea to do the dishes.

Although I didn't want to tiptoe about the chore, I did. What I wanted to do was bang dishes, slam cupboard drawers, and dammit, who wouldn't? But it wasn't *my* nature to carry on like a maniac.

Gillian was never open to anything new. We'd probably die living in this house, doing the same damn thing, day in, day out. And why she cared a lick about something that wouldn't even impact her, irritated the shit out of me.

What was the point of money if all it did was sit there? It didn't bring happiness – that was for damn sure – unless you used it on ideas that mattered to a person. I signed and unsuccessfully tried to unclench my jaw. Just because Gillian didn't understand the brilliance of my online boffer business idea didn't mean I wouldn't start doing some research.

As my wife continued to sit in the gathering darkness, I puttered around her kitchen – putting away the leftovers, depositing the wine bottles in the recycling bin, stacking the dirty dishes into the washer and turning it on. When I refer to it as *her kitchen*, it's not because I'm a chauvinist. I mean the kitchen is hers in the same way you would refer to any project someone had poured themselves into.

That's his university degree on the wall, or *that's her watercolour*. In that same way, the kitchen belongs to Gillian. I hadn't contributed anything. And besides, any ideas I'd offered had not been wanted.

I battled the baked-on cheese off the lasagne pan for several minutes before giving up. It was good enough. Because believe me, normally I'd just let that thing soak for a day or two. But that was sure to piss my wife off further.

As I dried the pan, ignoring the blackened bits which were now permanently part of it, I took one last look around the kitchen. There was nothing left to put away except the salt cellar. Bad memories, that salt.

Just looking at it caused my lungs to constrict. It conjured the afternoon I came home to find Gillian walking around our apparently outdated kitchen (news to me!) with an interior designer. The designer had been dressed in black, her hair pulled back in a severe pony tail, and her eyebrows tweezed into nonexistence. She'd not even bothered to remove her trench coat or shoes before traipsing through our home!

I watched as my wife lapped up everything Trench Coat suggested. They discussed raised panel versus shaker panel, nickel versus oil-rubbed bronze, the durability of granite countertops versus the timeless appearance of marble. Right. Who cares? It's a damn kitchen, not a palace. But I held my tongue. 'Cause that's what people do when they are trying to be supportive.

Gillian held up a booklet of paint samples. "What do you think of cloud white for the cabinets? Or could I get away with a dove grey without it dating too quickly? And open concept shelves instead of uppers. I want everything open."

"Definitely. Open shelving is a very modern look. But I'd consider a few upper cabinets... on this wall." The designer turned and pointed to the open space between our living room and kitchen. There was no wall in sight – then, at least. "Cloud white on these. It will make a great accent to the dove grey on the rest of your cabinets."

I cleared my throat. "I've always been partial to a dark cherry stain. Perhaps we could have these," and I felt a bit ridiculous, waving my arm in the air in reference to cabinets and a wall that didn't yet exist, "in a cherry wood stain." I smiled, looked from Gillian to the designer. They glanced at each other, but didn't otherwise respond to my suggestion. "It's just that paint colours come in and out of style."

"That's true," said Trench Coat, "and that's why it's so important to go with a hardwood cabinet. Hardwood can always be sanded down and repainted."

As if that made sense. How often did ordinary people refinish their cabinets? Not bloody often, I'd say. But Gillian nodded agreement.

Trench Coat looked down at her notes, assessing the list of must-haves. "Is there anything else you need to have in your kitchen? Remember, this is your space and you want it to work for you."

"We need some organization for spices. Oils. Vinegars. With our current set-up," and Gillian pulled open a cabinet jam-packed with every imaginable culinary spice, "everything is a mess. I can't find anything I need, when I need it. Even the salts – kosher, sea salt, table – there's got to be some kind of system that would keep this organised."

And when had that changed? When had two people started to need more than one kind of salt?

But like a lot of things, we hadn't talked about the salt.

I picked up the lone salt cellar and quietly opened the dove grey, custom-made, spice-pantry door and returned it to its proper place. Then changed my mind. Picked up that damn salt and hid it behind the olive oil.

Childish? Sure. But did it feel good?

You bet.

Chapter Seven

Dr Torres's hands rested on the glass desk that separated us. Supported by an angular chrome frame, the clear-as-crystal surface was free of smudges and fingerprints. Its transparency was blatant; it did not allow for secrets or hidden confidences. Especially not the kind one might be inclined to push to the back corner of a forgotten drawer. It didn't even allow for the unbuckling of a belt after a particularly filling lunch. It was not a desk I'd choose for myself.

"How did the homework go?" she asked expectantly.

"Not good?" My voice rose with uncertainty, making my statement sound more like a question then a firm answer. And perhaps it was. It was my best guess, taking into account the polite interactions between Ralph and me at Mr Singh's party and the disaster on Sunday as well as the last few days when we'd avoided any real conversation with each other. I'd alternately buried myself in sleep and in work. When I was focused on music, I didn't have to think. And when I was sleeping...let's just say it was difficult to get up after I lay down. My body was filled with lethargy and a heavy sensation I'd come to identify as low-grade hopelessness, if such a thing existed. "I tried. It's just hard to remain...civil sometimes."

"And what times are those?"

"The times when I'm disappointed."

Torres nodded her head as though I had said something to agree with. "It takes practice. A good deal of it. Open, communicative, and trusting marriages don't just happen. They take hard work. They aren't like a new romance where every morning dawns sunny. Where every night seems filled with playful bubble baths, fantastic sex and calorie-free ice cream."

"Uh, right." I didn't know how else to answer that one.

"Practice, Gillian. And finding solutions that work for both of you."

I knew what practice looked like from a musical perspective. For me, it involved playing a difficult section of music over and over until it felt like second nature. Is that how she was expecting us to improve our marriage, too? For us to practise being interested in each other until it happened without having to try? Oh God. That sounded completely horrible. It also sounded like something I'd have a lot of trouble following through on.

I sighed. "Perhaps I'd have better luck if I just cut my tongue out."

"Let's not do anything reckless quite yet," Torres said as she held her hands up. She was definitely a literal kind of person. "Why don't you tell me more about this past week? Could you give me an example of a particularly difficult situation? Perhaps a time you couldn't resist bringing up this hobby of his?"

I rambled out a broken account of Sunday, the day that had bloomed so hopeful but left me a larp widow. Even though it was obvious I deserved a giant F on my homework, I did not try to twist the tale with an overload of emotions and excuses. I was very mature and stuck to the facts. Facts like *I came home from yoga* and *the car was broken*.

If I hadn't been so conscientious, I might've sounded a bit more like this: *And then you know what that asshole does? He leaves me stranded at home. His old, haggard wife, all alone while he's out with his buddies participating in a moronic dress-up game.*

Okay. So what I mean is, I tried to be mature.

Other than a few clarifying questions, some throaty supportive sounds, and sporadic nodding, Torres didn't interrupt. She waited till I was done my tirade.

A moment of silence stretched between us. I used the

time to catch my breath and calm the agitated flush that splashed across my cheeks. Why was it so damn hot in here, anyway? I took off my cardigan and, with great deliberation, folded it over the side of my chair's armrest. My personal life was approaching the transparency of the glass desk, but it wasn't nearly as spotless.

"Thank you for sharing, Gillian." Torres cleared her throat, opened the notebook sitting in front of her, and flipped to a clean page. "When you tell me about the difficulties in your relationship, I get the distinct impression you don't feel as though you and Ralph are on the same... team, shall we say."

I nodded. "We don't seem to want the same things anymore."

"Yes, I can see why you'd say that. But I'm thinking it wasn't always like this. Otherwise, you'd have been sitting in that chair years ago." She pointed to the overstuffed armchair I was sitting in and smiled.

I watched her write the date and my name along the top of the paper before addressing me again. "So today, Gillian, I'm hoping you could tell me about another experience. This time, pick one from the past. I'd like to hear about a difficult time you and Ralph made it through together. A time when you felt the two of you were, indeed, on the same team."

"Er, sure." I searched my memory. "Any time?"

"Any time you think was significant."

My mind wandered back through the years to when my waist was trimmer, Ralph's hair fuller, and the future stretched out in front of us with promise. There was the time our apartment had flooded with the contents of a sewer backup. That was difficult. Or the time all our luggage had been lost en route to Cuba and we'd sat sweating in the same clothes for three days. It had been a challenge we'd tackled with several icy beverages, hand soap, the bathroom sink, and good humour.

We'd worked together in supporting Jas and Arianna when Keith had died. It had been traumatic. The result of a sudden car crash on the way home from work. It had altered life instantaneously for my dear friend and her daughter, who'd only been a child. Their grief, and ours, had absolutely resulted in Ralph and me pulling together as a team, there was no doubt of that.

But perhaps because of our recent fight, I'd spent the last few days thinking about the choice we'd made to move to Calgary. The move had allowed me to accept an offer of employment with the Philharmonic Orchestra.

"Early in our marriage, we made a pretty big decision to leave Ontario and move here. To Calgary." This seemed as good an example as any. "It meant leaving friends and family. Ralph had to quit his job, which was something he agreed to do for my career. We just decided, and the next day we started packing everything up. Within a month, we'd left our old life behind.

"I'd been offered this great position with the Calgary Philharmonic Orchestra – Associate Principal Horn – that's kind of like second best. It was an exciting accomplishment, especially for someone my age. Before that, I'd been piecing work together freelance in Toronto – travelling shows like Cirque, some coaching and teaching students, really whatever came along. But this position with the Orchestra, it was a big break for me."

Thinking about my younger self was something I usually avoided. It gave me this weird disconnected feeling, as though I'd cut the strings between the younger me and the current me. Back then, I'd been driven by my career. I'd wanted to succeed and travel the world with my horn. But I'd misplaced that passion somewhere. First one career opportunity then another would come up. I would smile, thank them, and shake my head. I'd let them slide by until I was no longer asked.

And I'd been completely fine with it. I'd assumed life would take a new direction. But that had dead-ended somehow.

And now, here I was: third horn and I couldn't care less about the world stage. I cleared my throat and, for Torres's benefit, skipped all the tedious humdrum.

"Anyway, it was an exciting time for me. And Ralph had stood beside me, even though it had meant giving up a lot of the security and comforts we'd had back east. It definitely felt like we were a team."

Torres leaned back in her chair, regarding me. "Could you tell me a bit about the adjustment after you moved?"

"Well, for the first few months every day seemed to bring some new adventure. All the little things you take for granted – like getting your hair cut. It was misery trying to find someone who could cut curly hair without making me look like an adult version of Annie. But we'd laugh about it and I'd try somewhere new. Or trying to find a coffee shop – one that played decent music. Back home there'd been lots of places you could just sit and read without people wondering why you weren't buying doughnuts." I smiled, thinking how this had unfortunately led to a personal addiction to apple fritters. "The worst part was probably missing our old friends and trying to make new ones. But we persevered because we'd made a choice. It would be just Ralph and me, and that would be enough."

"And was it enough?"

"It was. For a long time, it was enough."

A few minutes went by before Torres asked me anything else. "When you remember back to that period of time, can you pinpoint what made you feel, 'hey, we weathered that storm together?' Because I heard you say you decided it would be just Ralph and you. It definitely sounds like you were on the same team."

I lifted my eyebrows and tilted my head to the side as I thought about what she'd said. "You're right. It did feel that way." But what had it been that made us feel that way? Well, there was the obvious. "For starters, we weren't at each other's throats all the time. We seemed to be...I don't know...just in it together rather than each going our own way. And, well, we had hope for the future."

Torres nodded. "In it together," she said, repeating my words. Leaning forward over the glass desk, she reminded me of someone enthralled with a movie they were watching. It made me smile. I was certain my life was not that exciting. I glanced behind her at the clock. Wow. The session was nearly over and I hadn't noticed.

"Are you ready for your homework?"

Hesitantly, I nodded. Last week's assignment had gone offline, but I saw no better option than to try again.

"I believe that no relationship lasts long when there aren't any shared interests and there isn't any fun. Otherwise, you will find it elsewhere." She gave me a long look over the top of her purples frames. "Gillian, I'd like to tell you a story about friends of mine. One partner has always enjoyed golfing. The other partner had lived her entire life without golf and would have been happy to live the rest without ever understanding what a bogey was.

"From the time the snow melts until the courses close down in the fall, this guy is out on the greens three out of four weekends. And in the winter, he's hightailing it to Arizona for a golf vacation if he can swing it."

"Sounds...lopsided."

"True. And my friend had a choice." Torres held out her left hand and held up her pointer finger. "She could complain bitterly and be miserable." A second finger shot up to represent the second option. "She could swallow her feelings and pretend it didn't bug her." Predictably, a third finger was raised. "She could leave him. Just give up and walk away." Torres's pinky finger unfolded. "Or she could do something completely bizarre. She could check out what all the excitement was about golf." I was now staring at four fingers, outlining her friend's four options for dealing with her golf-addicted spouse. "Do you know what she did?"

"Left him?" I was kind of joking and I kind of wasn't. Even if I hadn't verbalised it to anyone, this was the action I'd started contemplating. The secret I'd tucked away in the back corner of a dark drawer. Hidden, perhaps, but not forgotten.

"She took golf lessons."

I smiled tentatively. "Well, um, that's nice." Now here

was a course of action I'd certainly not been considering.

"You're right. It was nice. In fact, it was an opportunity to inject a little goodwill into her marriage." Torres gave me another meaningful look over the rim of her frames. Right. Last week's homework. This friend was obviously a more diligent student than I. "Do you know, Gillian, what she discovered through this choice?"

"What a bogey was?"

It was clear my humour was wasted on Torres.

"She discovered that even though golf was not her favourite activity, it wasn't torture either. Some weekends she does her own thing, and some weekends she joins him on the green. They talk more. They laugh more. Afterward, they often make dinner together. And sometimes they even follow that up with some great sex."

"Wow. It sounds better than a bogey."

"The point is, Gillian, being open to try something new has brought them closer together." Torres pressed her hands together in illustration of her concept. "Golfing will never be my friend's favourite activity. But she can do it, and she can find some enjoyment in it. Best of all, by being open to trying something her partner loves, she has brought good energy and connection into her marriage."

I didn't know what to say about the golf per say, but something else was clicking. Golf was obviously a metaphor for something else. Something significant. Which meant the story must be a parable or allegory of some sort.

My heart lurched. Of course. I took a deep breath. "It's because we don't have any children. Because I just know it would've been different if we'd had kids. Children bring people together, like a team." I brought my own palms together in illustration. "It's a common interest. Just like golf."

Torres's smile faltered. "No, Gillian. It's not like golf. Too often, children are the glue in strained marriages, and that is an unfair expectation to place on them. Besides, divorce is just as common in families with children as in those without children, wouldn't you agree?"

50

"I suppose. I just have always felt that if we'd had kids…"

"But you don't. You've got Ralph, and he has you."

Leaning back, Torres rested her elbows on the arms of her chair and tented her fingertips in a pyramid. "I am sure you're following me, Gillian, but just to be clear: The golf is not about the golf. And the golf is not about kids. In this instance, golf is about the marriage. I'd like you to try to consider this: Ralph has found an activity he is passionate about."

No. The golf was supposed to represent something significant. It had to!

"Gillian, I am hearing you say that you and Ralph don't spend quality time together. You feel more like disgruntled roommates than intimate partners. True?"

I nodded weakly.

"For your homework, let me present you with a challenge: Why not be open to this live-action thing? Who knows? It may make you smile. It may make you laugh. It may even improve your sex life. How terrible could it be?"

Chapter Eight

Rolling through the last bars of a sweeping crescendo, the final sounds of Tolkien's middle earth rang out through the concert hall. I imagined the sound waves rippling out from the brightly lit stage, washing over the audience sitting in the darkness before reverberating off the Carthy organ, its pipes immense and linear behind the orchestra. The night's performance was *Adventures in Fantasy and Sci-Fi*, one of the 'fun performances' tailored to bring classical music to the current generation.

As silence filled the hall, I kept my eye on the conductor, waiting for the cue to lower our instruments. He continued to hold his baton aloft for several seconds before lowering it, and in unison, we lowered our various instruments to a resting position. The audience, still hidden in darkness, came alive with thunderous applause. It was only then I allowed my mind to settle on thoughts unconnected to the music.

In particular, I wondered how the evening might be going for my guests. I peered into the bright lights and applauding crowd in the general direction of the mezzanine. Even though I couldn't see them, I knew Ralph, Jas, and our new acquaintance, Bendar, were seated there (or standing, as it were; the audience was currently getting to its feet for a standing ovation). I grimaced at the thought of the text messages I was sure would be waiting for me on my phone. I'd meant to give Jas the heads up about Bendar joining – I truly had – but since my session with Torres, I'd mentally deflated.

I pulled my thoughts back to the piece we'd planned for an encore – the triumphant opening sequence to the *Star*

Trek: The Next Generation television series – and got back to work.

When we'd truly finished, taken our bows, gathered our sheet music and instruments, nodded goodbye to colleagues, and exited the stage, I escaped through the side door and into the lobby. That's where Ralph and Jas usually waited for me, and sure enough, they were both there. As was Bendar.

Bendar happened to be the only one who looked up as I manoeuvred my French horn case through the tight doorway, and I smiled in greeting. Jas's head was down as she thumbed out a text with furious speed, and Ralph was speaking to a woman whose back was to me. Her hair, piled high in a loose bun, and her scooped-back neckline helped me immediately place her: the flutist-*slash*-larper. Great. I gritted my teeth, trying to remember her name. Lisa? Laura? I'd kind of made it a point not to go out of my way getting to know her.

She always sat a few rows in front of me. Other than careful head nods when we happened to make eye contact, I tried my best to avoid her. I knew it was childish. In the extreme. But I couldn't help blaming her for the whole larp craze that had made a fiasco out of my marriage.

Besides, I could not remember an unattractive flutist. Case in point: tonight. Although the whole orchestra were required to wear black for performances, the meltingly seductive melodies of the woodwind musicians somehow seemed to match their personal dress style. Bare-shouldered, asymmetrical necklines or the most luxurious textured scarfs.

I'd tried, but never mastered that art. I was wearing my usual black cashmere turtleneck and dress pants. A lengthy silver necklace and chunky pendant were my only embellishments. Instinctively, I reached up and clasped the pendant in my hand. It had been a gift from Ralph, purchased on our first road trip into the Rockies after we'd moved west.

We'd marvelled at the proximity of the mountains. Only

one hour, and pine-covered peaks were soaring around you. Those were quickly overtaken by even higher summits, which rose above where any tree could grow, their crevices home to ancient, crystal-white glaciers.

Banff, our destination on that first trip, was a mecca for both tourists and students looking for work. We parked in the bustling town centre and joined them with enthusiasm, our map – covered in bear-encounter facts – and 35-millimetre camera. Halfway down the main street, we come to a shop specialising in Indigenous art. I remembered walking in and immediately becoming interested in a showcase of silver-plated Haida jewellery.

Each ring, pendant and broach bore an engraving of a totem animal etched in silver. For the benefit of the customers, simple definitions were listed beside each animal. My eyes scanned over the various animals – Bear, Wolf, Raven – when they stopped on Dragonfly.

Sitting on a bed of deep navy velvet, the Dragonfly's slender silver-winged body was placed directly above the words *Transformation and Change*. And below that was this explanation:

First Nations people of the Northwest Coast believe the Dragonfly to be a creature adaptable to change. The Dragonfly's swift flight and its ability to move in all six directions radiate a sense of power and control amidst a constantly moving environment. He is a symbol of transformation, and he gains his stability from the mental and emotional maturity that develops alongside a deeper understanding of the meaning of life.

I traced the delicately etched double wings before leaving it behind. The price was steep, and Ralph and I had budgeted only for lunch in the park and a trip up Sulphur Mountain on the gondola.

Atop the mountain later that afternoon, the wind whipped my ill-cut hair in all directions.

"You're beautiful," Ralph said, squeezing my hand, and I

laughed. I'd been trying fruitlessly to hold my hair back with one hand, the other warm in Ralph's grasp as we walked the tourist pathway at the top of the ridge.

Ralph stopped another tourist and asked if she would take our picture. The stranger kindly obliged, snapping a picture of our laughing faces, the majestic Rockies stretched out behind us.

After thanking her, Ralph pulled me against the rail and kissed me, my hair whipping around us both in a mad cloud. It was then Ralph pressed the silver dragonfly pendant into the palm of my hand.

I released the dragonfly, letting my hand drop. It felt an ancient memory now. I needed to focus on the present.

I turned towards Bendar, who looked a bit unsure what to do with himself. I couldn't blame him, what with an angry texter on one side and a pair of larpers on the other.

"So?" I said, extending my hand in greeting. "What did you think?"

"Amazing. Honestly. Truly inspiring."

My forced smile turned into a genuine grin at his enthusiasm. "I'm glad you enjoyed it."

Jas looked up from her phone and then shoved it into her purse. "Well done! Once again, well done, Gill!" She pulled me into a hug and used the opportunity to hiss in my ear. "Could've told me!"

"It couldn't have been that bad," I whispered back. "Besides, I kind of forgot."

We chatted about my time with the orchestra as well as Bendar's own high school experiences playing in the band. Jas, arms crossed and foot tapping, was useless at helping keep the conversation going. By the time we'd exhausted the topic of which science fiction movies we'd all seen, I'd already shot several looks over at Ralph. I frowned. How much was there to talk about?

I turned back to our guests and asked, "Do you have time for a glass of wine? Ralph, we should have some wine."

"Thank you, but I've already had a glass," replied Bendar just as Jas said, "Sorry, got to go check on Arianna and her homework."

"Right. Yes, of course." I cleared my throat. I was done waiting patiently. I tapped Ralph on the shoulder. "Dear, we need to say goodbye to our guests. It's nice to see you" – jeez, what was her name again? – "Laura."

"Lauren." Ralph corrected.

"Right. Okay, well, see you." I nodded farewell, my hand on Ralph's forearm, ready to pull him away. But apparently he wasn't quite finished his conversation.

"I'll be right with you, Gill."

I – what? Had he just...? Wow. I plastered on a smile and stiffly turned back to my guests. Which happened to now be one guest.

"Your friend went to the coat check," Bendar informed me. I nodded. My irritation at Ralph must have been evident because he leaned forward, hands in pockets, and said, "I was married once." I nodded again, unsure what to say to that. But nothing was necessary because he continued by saying, "It's not easy."

A lopsided grin crossed my face despite my frustration with Ralph. "It certainly isn't. But what is?"

"Certainly not being single."

"And why is that?"

"Everyone assumes you must be looking for a woman. They can't imagine a man being content without one."

I laughed. He was practically a stranger, yet he could see my unhappiness. He shook my hand goodbye, then Ralph's, as my derelict husband had finally decided to join us. He inclined his head towards Jas, who was just returning with her crème spring trench coat in hand.

"Ben," she said, not bothering to extend her hand but instead giving a hard smile that didn't reach her eyes.

"Jas."

Bendar walked away and Ralph left to visit the restroom, giving Jas and me a few minutes to ourselves.

"Can you believe that guy?" Jas was fuming. Her

56

shoulders were rigid and she was practically grinding her teeth in irritation. "He asked where my husband was!"

I glanced down at Jas's wedding rings. She still wore them on occasion, which I thought was sweet and very sentimental but definitely sent a certain message. "Well, I could see how a person might jump to that conclusion. And, ah…didn't you ask about his wife and children the first time we met? Touché, perhaps?"

"No, he was trying to tell me…I don't know, but something. Something like, 'You have a child so you should have a husband.'"

"Are you sure?"

"Of course, I'm sure! I know what goes on in my own culture."

I took a deep breath. "You are wearing a wedding ring."

Jas thought about that for a moment. "Well, yes. He obviously has no principles, either." Jas leaned towards me. "I informed him I was a widow. And then you know what he does, not five minutes later? Offers to buy me a drink!"

"When was this?"

"During the intermission."

I looked around the lobby. The overpriced bar was still open, as I knew it had been during the intermission. People stood around in small groups or meandered over to the coat check, glasses of wine and beer in their hands.

"A lot of people are enjoying drinks. Jas, I think you're reading a little too much into this one. Maybe he was simply offering to buy you a drink because it was polite."

Jas wrinkled her nose. "I know what happened, Gill. And I'm not interested."

"Don't take it the wrong way, but I don't think he's interested either. I kind of got the impression he wasn't looking for a relationship right now."

Jas's eyebrows shot up her forehead in surprise. "Why? What did he say?"

I shrugged my shoulders. "I don't know. Something like, 'Your friend thinks I'm interested, but I don't go for single parents who wear wedding rings.'"

"What! Oh my God, seriously?"

I laughed. "Of course not. He said something like, 'Marriage. Hard work. Not fun.'" I grimaced. "I couldn't disagree."

Jas was immediately sympathetic. "How are things going, by the way?"

"Oh, same as usual." I cleared my throat. "But I did have another session with that counsellor. She gave me some more homework." I whispered the basic plan to Jas. Torres's quality-time plan. It still didn't sound sane, even in my own words.

"What?" Jas said, grabbing my wrist after I'd given her the gist of it. "Okay, we need to talk."

But it was then that Ralph had made his way back, weaving through the slowly departing crowd. There was no time to expand on the conversation further. "Ready to go, ladies?"

We walked together to the parking lot, then Ralph and I said goodbye to Jas.

I stopped mid-stride, on the edge of the parking lot, looking left and right and not seeing our vehicle. I'd arrived in a taxi, as I needed to be at the concert hall several hours before the audience. "Where did you park the car?" I snapped.

"Right there, Gillian." He pointed. Sure enough, my Camry was within eyesight. Without thanking him, I headed in that direction at a fast clip. I heard him press the unlock button behind me, and as I got to the car the trunk opened as if by its own accord. I placed my French horn inside, slammed the lid closed, then proceeded to get in through the passenger side door.

Ralph got into the driver's seat a little more slowly. Shutting the door, he held the keys in his hand but didn't start the vehicle. He turned to me.

"Look, Gill. About the other night. I didn't mean—"

"It's fine."

Ralph sighed and rubbed his eyes. "We should try and talk about this."

"Honestly, it's fine. I'm just tired. A little on edge." I gave him a weak smile. I didn't have the energy to fight right now. All I wanted was to go home and sleep. "Anyway, what's going on with your vehicle?"

"They had to replace the starter; no big deal. I'll pick it up from the shop tomorrow. I need it for…well, for next weekend."

I didn't bother asking what was happening next weekend, and he didn't bother expanding. Because we both already knew.

Chapter Nine

"Is it that hard for you to support me on this?" I could feel the tension in my voice and knew Jas could hear it too. My arms were tightly crossing my chest, and with some effort, I relaxed my shoulders and dropped my hands to my lap.

"I'm sorry," said Jas, trying to settle me. "It's just…are you sure this therapist is…I don't know…accredited?"

"Accredited?"

"I'm not sure what it's called, but you know what I mean." Jas had stopped in for tea under the pretence she happened to be in the neighbourhood, but I didn't believe her. She'd spent the whole visit hedging around my coming trip down larp lane, and I hadn't been exactly forthcoming. She'd apparently decided to switch to a more direct line of questioning. "Are you sure this therapist is legit? Because the homework she gave you seems…unusual."

I took a sip of my now-lukewarm tea. "My benefit plan seems to think she's legitimate. They only pay certified professionals."

"Hmm." Jas didn't look convinced. "But maybe a second opinion might not hurt?"

If I had the energy, I might seek out a second opinion. But I didn't. I'd spent the last few days in a fog, my emotional reserves depleted. I knew Jas's concerns were valid – the homework seemed the equivalent of half-baked horseshit – but I'd made a decision to stick to the prescribed course. "Look, Jas, I'm going."

"Let me get this straight: you don't think it'll work, and yet you're still going?"

I set my cup down. What felt like a migraine was closing in on my temples. "I've tried everything."

"Have you?"

"Maybe."

"Do you still love him?"

"Sure, I love him. Of course. In a very ambivalent, life-is-not-what-I'd-planned sort of way. Most days we don't even talk. We live in the same house, Jas, and there's nothing there." I took a deep breath, trying to calm myself. "And that's why I'm following through with this insane plan: because I'm out of normal, sane options. And if it doesn't work," I took a deep breath and hastily spit out the rest before I could change my mind, "then I can walk away. With a clear conscious."

There. I'd said it. Finally. I'd said aloud what had been lurking silently in my thoughts.

The seconds ticked by. Again, Jas was the first to say something.

"If going to a role-play game in order to make a life-altering decision about your marriage were a good idea, I'd get behind you on this, Gill. But it just seems," her eyes wandered around my kitchen, looking for some type of inspiration, and she found it, "it seems like you have your way of avoiding things and Ralph has his."

"Are you suggesting renovating my ugly seventies kitchen was avoiding something?" Every muscle in my jaw was clenched. "You know that we'd always planned on doing it. It has nothing, whatsoever, to do with it. Besides, not everyone handles things the way you do."

"I know. I'm just saying—"

"Well, it's not the same." I shut my mouth, biting off the rest of my words. I wanted to say our situation wasn't like hers and Keith's. But there are things that aren't easy to take back.

"I care about you, Gill. You know that. I'm not talking about custom cabinets or the search for perfect hardware. I'm not even talking about going to this larp thing." I could feel Jas's eyes searching my face for a crack. I wasn't giving it to her. "I'm talking about staying so busy – pursuing all kinds of hobbies and projects – just so you

61

don't need to stop and process what happened."

Silence blanketed me in a sheet of ice, freezing out any response I could possibly give.

The doorbell rang.

I turned away from my friend and went to answer the door. Canvassers for a noble cause. My mind didn't register the disease they were hoping to cure or the social issue they were raising funds to address. Instead, I handed them the lone twenty-dollar bill that happened to be sitting in my wallet and wished them well.

When I returned to the kitchen, Jas was putting our empty teacups in the sink. I sat down at the table.

"I'm tired, Jas. I'm just not...I think I need to lie down," I said.

Jas drew a breath and let it out before responding. "Are you mad at me?"

I shook my head. "Nah." I looked away. "Maybe." I looked back at her and gave her a tired smile. "A little," I admitted.

"I'm worried about you." Jas reached down to where I sat in the chair and gave me a hug about the shoulders. "But you know I'm not going to lie to you."

I managed to nod so she knew I'd heard her.

Jas left and I turned off the kitchen lights, headed straight to my bedroom, and closed the curtains. Crawling into bed, I took refuge under the heavy quilt. And tried not to dream.

Chapter Ten

I woke to an empty house. Looking at the time, I realised Ralph must have left for work at least two hours earlier. I had a practice later in the afternoon with the horn section, but for now I had plenty of time to wallow around in my pyjamas, my morning lethargy, and my nagging self-doubt. Coffee was sure to make good company for all three.

I'd been in bed since Jas had left the evening before. And although I'd slept soundly, my mind had not been at ease. I knew she'd made some good arguments. She might even be right. Of course she was right. But this was no longer about right. It was about moving forward. I dragged myself out of bed, stumbled over to the window, and opened the curtains. Warm rays of sun streamed into the bedroom and I raised my arms above my head and stretched.

If I was truly serious about following through on Torres's plan, I might as well start putting the idea into action. I went downstairs to the kitchen, making a detour to our home office for our laptop, and brewed myself some strong coffee.

It wasn't hard to find the live-action club Ralph belonged to. Although the business card in our laundry room was no longer around, there were other ways. Neither of us kept passwords on our home email accounts so it was easy to peruse his account for the latest larp update, then search for the club name on the Internet. And, *bam*! There it was. I sipped my coffee and did what any curious person would do first.

I watched their YouTube video. It depicted a battle, and it was as I expected: boffer weapons, costumes, and the great outdoors. What I hadn't expected: people chanting stuff like *normal blow four, normal blow four* and *killing blow one, killing blow two, killing blow three* as they enacted a mock fight. Hmmm. No one was laughing. No one was even grinning. I wondered how they could stay so serious.

Somewhat relieved not to have seen my husband in the video, I closed the YouTube window and went back to the club website. A list of upcoming gaming dates and links to costume suppliers – *is this where Ralph plans to advertise his boffer-business scheme?* I meant to read up about the club, but the site contained several photos of people posing in costumes and I was easily distracted. I zoomed in on one.

Why was that man holding his hands six inches above someone else's head? Was it some type of pretend curse? I gritted my teeth. This was…perhaps not going to work. No matter what Torres thought – my God, was that cleavage for real? – larp was *not* golf.

Okay, I'd tried. Against both my and Jas's better judgement, I'd at least been open to the idea. I could tell Torres I had gone as far as checking out the larp website and watching some battle videos, but experiencing all this in person? No. I couldn't wrap my head around it. Torres was welcome to check it out herself if she thought it was no big deal. I laughed, visualising my very proper therapist in armour, hollering *kill blow one, kill blow two!*

My mind made up, I was about to click the mouse on the red *X* in the top right-hand corner of the screen, forever shutting down this idiotic idea, when my hand stilled. I spotted an announcement that had previously escaped my attention:

NON-PLAYER-CHARACTERS (NPC) NEEDED

Don't have a costume but enjoy cosplay?
Come out to camp as a NPC!
Join our monster camp and bring a
new villain to life every day.
Use of our costumes and makeup included.

This is your chance to experience live-action
excitement at an affordable price!

If that had been it, there was no doubt I'd have turned the website off instantly. But below was another announcement:

VOLUNTEER KITCHEN NPCs NEEDED

Enjoy a live-action weekend for free.
The comfort of heated bunks, flush
toilets, and hot meals included.
What we need from you:
Assistance preparing meals with our
friendly community of kitchen wenches.
Discounts available for those needing to rent costumes.

My hand froze over the mouse as a plan began to percolate.

Chapter Eleven

I woke on Sunday morning to the sound of my phone pinging. A text from Jas, reminding me about yoga. Was I still in? I was. It had been two days since I'd seen her, and in that time I had not done much that could be considered productive. I'd taken care of my basic hygiene. Attended work when I had to.

I'd also spent ridiculous amounts of time creeping the larp website, and had watched endless seasons of long dead television sitcoms on Netflix. In my spare moments I'd fought off a migraine, or perhaps it had just been an immense shadow of dread. I didn't know for sure; they both felt equally painful, and something to be avoided. And so I quietly gathered my yoga belongings, Ralph as usual still fast asleep this time on a Sunday morning, and headed out.

I was in the lobby, assessing the state of my toenail polish, when Jas arrived and sat down on the bench beside me.

"Are they bad?" I pointed to my toenails.

Jas looked down to assess the state of my feet. "Ummm, no one will notice."

"Right." I unfortunately never remembered my feet until they were on display for public exposure. I liked to believe that yoga types were too Zen to be judging my gnarly feet in the same way I tried to believe ice cream wouldn't make the waist band on my pants tighter.

"So…I've been thinking about what you said."

Oh, great. Jas was getting right back into it. I sighed, steeling myself up inside. "Honey, I just cannot have this conversation again."

"I know. I'm sorry – I just wanted to remind you that

I've got your back. I don't have to necessarily agree with you in order to have your back, right?"

I smiled, feeling a sense of relief. "True." I leaned my head against my friend's shoulder, and she gave me a playful pat before we entered the studio.

"I've got your back, but not got your feet. There are limits to friendship, you know."

I laughed. They were pretty bad. Jas's perfectly pedicured feet looked like a magazine advertisement next to my mad mess of cracked heels and calluses. But as we sat down on our mats, the sun streaming through the windows and the AC already pouring out the air circulation vent in our favourite corner, I stuck my feet out for the world to see. There were worse things.

"I've just been wondering about one thing. What does Ralph think about you crashing his hobby?"

I turned so I could look Jas straight in the eye and get her full reaction, already preparing myself to watch her cringe. "I'm actually thinking of not telling Ralph. I might just surprise him out there, at the camp."

Jas bit her lip. "That might turn out...romantic." Her tone of voice didn't sound very convincing, but I knew she was trying and that was all I could ask for. It's not as if I thought the plan was stellar either.

"Aren't you funny! Actually, I'm thinking Torres might not approve: I'm only surprising Ralph if, when I get out to this live-action thing, I can in any way see myself doing this. Then I'll be like, 'Hey, Ralph. I support you. Let's enjoy some quality time together playing your pretend game.' But if it's just too much and I can't, I'll pack up and leave the proverbial golf course behind. No harm done."

"And how are you going to manage that?"

The practice room was filling up with other participants, and a plethora of multicoloured mats now surrounded us. I lowered my voice. The whole larp thing embarrassed me, in a similar way to having your skirt tucked into the back of your underwear or discovering lettuce stuck between your teeth several hours after lunch. "I was on the website for the live-action group that Ralph belongs to. They've got a request out for volunteers. To help in the kitchen."

"Volunteers?"

"By volunteers it sounds like they mean kitchen wenches. Essentially."

Jas had been in the process of taking a sip from her water bottle, and she coughed. I gave her a firm slap on her back to help keep her from choking.

"Pardon me?"

"In order for these live-action things to work, they need a bunch of supporting cast, or whatever. People to move props, and people for," I looked around quickly to make sure no one was listening and lowered my voice even more, "monster camp, and people to, like, feed people. All the participants need to eat. You basically wear sassy clothes from the Middle Ages and keep the hearth warm and roast pig and mutton. And, well, you know. Wash dishes."

Jas, for once, didn't seem to have a quick response. But her expression said enough. She had forgotten to close her mouth and she looked, for lack of a better word, flabbergasted. I wondered if this was too much for her and if the conversation would revert back to the one we'd had in my kitchen the other day. I held my breath and rushed on.

"I know, Jas, I know. It's insane. It goes against everything I believe about gender roles. But this is the beauty of it: I can go undercover, cook some goddamn chicken on a spit, and check it out without making a commitment I can't keep. If it looks like something that I could stomach doing maybe once or twice a year, then I'll pursue it. It's like golf, right? Give a little, hopefully get something I want out of it."

"What do you want to get out of it?"

I shrugged. "A relationship with a little more connection than the one I have with our yoga instructor?" We both looked up towards the woman who led our Sunday yoga class. She was currently setting up props at the front of the room. My relationship with her was very surface. *Am I doing this position correctly?*, *How was your holiday?*, and

68

I love your new tank top! basically summed up our history. This was certainly fine for an instructor you saw once a week. It wasn't so great for someone you were supposed to be sharing a life with.

"Right." Jas took another sip of her water before screwing the cap back on and placing it at the end of her mat. "And if it doesn't work?"

I clasped my hands around my folded knees and pressed my lips together. "Then it doesn't. Like I said before, I'll have tried everything."

"You won't have tried *monster camp.*" Jas burst into laughter. "I'm sorry, I couldn't help it."

"Very funny." But I smiled too. "That's one thing I'm not doing."

Jas looked a little stunned, and I didn't blame her. I could barely comprehend myself that my continued marriage to Ralph depended on the success of a weekend of larping, for God's sake. A minute or two crept by and still she hadn't said anything.

"What? Just say it," I said in the hushed tones associated with public yoga studios.

"It's, um, not quite in the spirit that your therapist suggested. But, um, ya. It's totally you. In a very weird, very intense sort of way." She reached over and squeezed my arm. "I hope it works, Gill. I really do. And if not, then like you said, you'll know. When will you…embark on your journey?"

"Friday night. I've already taken the plunge and signed up."

"Wow, you go, girl."

I felt a level of anxiety lift off my chest. I was putting my plan into action, and I had my best friend's endorsement, which meant, to me, that I couldn't be completely losing my mind on this scheme. Who knew? Maybe it would be surprisingly romantic?

Because I was so fixated on my own thoughts, it took me a few moments to realise Jas was trying to get my attention. As I met her gaze, she made a quick flicking gesture with her chin. I turned to the left, the general direction her chin had indicated, and did a quick visual scan. Nothing seemed unexpected or unusual. I looked back at Jas.

"What?" I mouthed. She again flicked her head in the same direction, and this time her eyeballs seemed fixed on a man, lying flat out on his back in corpse pose. He looked familiar, but for a second I couldn't quite place him.

As if on cue, he sat up and moved directly into a forward bend. His hands wrapped around the bottom of his feet. Impressive. As were the toned muscles in his back and shoulders, which I could see through the tight fabric of his fitted athletic shirt. It was none other than Jas's sexy yoga partner from last week.

I turned my head away before the other participants caught me staring. Overt gazing, except between your toes, at your navel, or with your inner eye was considered something of a no-no at yoga. (The whole concept of a third eye mystified me. It was apparently located mid-forehead and, if working 20/20, was enlightening and not at all cyclops-ish. It was also, apparently, a no-no to giggle when an instructor led an inner-eye meditation).

I smiled at Jas, my eyebrows shooting up in anticipation. She was grinning, and under her dark mocha complexion, I swore there was a warm blush flushing her cheeks. I was glad that one of us had some excitement in our lives.

Brass cymbals chimed at the front of the room. This was the signal the class was about to begin, and sure enough, the instructor sat down on her own mat and welcomed the participants. "I'm glad you chose to get up on this rainy morning and share your practice with me. Let's take a few minutes in a simple cross-legged position to focus our minds and find our breath."

Out of my peripheral vision, I saw Daniel move out of his forward bend and into a crossed-legged position. He then turned his head towards us, looking directly at Jas as though I weren't there. As though he knew he would find her there all along. Sure enough, his face showed no surprise. He kept his gaze overtly on Jas, nodded in

70

greeting, and winked.

Jas, my completely competent, no-nonsense friend, was immediately flustered. A smile spread across my own face as I slowly backed up to encourage a direct line of sight between the two of them. If yoga wasn't enough to distract me from my impending collision with wench costumes, this should do it.

After class I waited by Jas's car. Although my body was hidden behind the van parked beside my friend's vehicle, I had a clear visual through the studio's floor-to-ceiling windows. Daniel and Jas had been chatting in the lobby for at least five minutes now. My friend seemed to be laughing. A lot. I wondered if he was awfully funny or if she was overly giddy. Daniel would say something, and Jas would laugh while using her fingertips to touch the space below her collarbones or to tuck wisps of silky black hair behind her ear, and even, once, to touch Daniel's forearm.

Jas? Who was this person? I couldn't remember ever seeing her flirt with a man. Certainly not in any of the years since her husband had died.

As Jas left the yoga studio and waved farewell to Daniel, I pushed thoughts of Keith out of my mind. We'd spent five years focused more or less on saying goodbye to Keith, and I saw no reason to bring him up at this moment.

Jas skipped towards me. Her footsteps, light with joy, were practically shooting her up off the asphalt with each step. "Can you believe that guy? He must be two percent body fat, if that," she said, quickly checking over her shoulder for a last glimpse.

"No doubt, he's beautiful. But what's he like?"

"Completely charming. Very funny." Jas blew out her cheeks and slowly let the air out. "My aging body is overheating from all this attention."

I laughed. "Your aging body is only a couple years older than mine. Besides, you're beautiful."

"Thanks."

Jas was wearing brightly patterned capris and a fitted

tank top with built-in sports bra. I'd long been envious that she managed to look curvy and fit at the same time. I wished I had that problem. As usual, I'd paired my black leggings with a loose top intended to hide my boxy boy figure. My frame had slowly been gaining flesh as I'd aged, but it had somehow not translated into curves.

"I saw you dig out your phone. Did you exchange numbers?"

"Yip. I've officially done it, Gill! I'm heading into the world of dating."

I put my arm around her shoulder. "Congrats! It looks... very exciting."

A guilty look washed over Jas's features, which is certainly not what I'd wanted. "I'm sorry if you haven't felt I've been very supportive of your plan. I guess I'm just worried. I love you. You know that, right?"

"I know. Love you too." But although I didn't admit it to her, it seemed to me our lives were going in two very different directions. I was slumping about in scuffed-up hiking boots. Jas was dazzling in three-inch heels. At that moment, I couldn't help but wish I were in her shoes.

"I'm headed to Arianna's swim practice. Do you want to join me?"

I smiled. Ever one to put off uncomfortable tasks, it seemed to me my errand could wait a little longer. "Sure. I'll follow you over."

The lanes were teaming with young swimmers. Brightly coloured caps bobbed up and down, travelling back and forth across the pool. And yet Arianna stood out like a beacon to me: lean brown arms and legs moving in a self-possessed rhythm. Not rushed. Not exhausted. Not fighting for every breath. She was as fluid as the water around her. She gave the impression that swimming the front crawl was the easiest thing in the world.

Right.

Gawd, I hated exercise.

"When did she get so...grown-up?" I said, turning and

looking at Jas. My friend's eyes were riveted on her daughter and a look of parental pride was easily readable on her face.

"Heck if I know. It seems we were just going to DQ for sundaes last week, chocolate sauce a mad-mess all over her chin."

I watched as Arianna, a fingertip away from the end of her lane, folded herself into a somersault and used her feet to kick off the wall of the pool, cleanly dolphin-kicking her body back in the direction she'd just travelled. Her blue-capped head briefly emerged from the water, and then once again she was face down, moving across the length of the pool.

"Sheesh, I'm sweating and I'm just watching." I peeled off my coat and placed it beside Jas's which she had already taken off. Although the temperature was cool outdoors, it was humid and hot sitting on the stands on the pool deck.

"Mom! Gill!" Arianna had stopped for a breather between laps and was waving to us. We waved, then seeing her beckon for us to come over, we carefully navigated down the stands and onto the deck floor.

"You're looking great," I said.

"Thanks Aunty!"

"Do you need something, honey?" Jas cast an eye at the mounds of matching swim club bags for her daughter's. "Change of goggles? Water bottle?"

"No. I'm good. I'm going out with my friends after practice, remember? We are going to a movie and I'm taking the bus home. So you know…you don't need to stay."

"Oh. Right. The movie. Is that today?" Jas said, trying to regain her footing in the conversation. She looked suddenly unsure of herself. "We'll just watch you swim and then go home, honey. Or do you want me to drive you and your friends to the theatre? I could do that. No problem."

Arianna's brow scrunched up, causing her silicone cap to wrinkle with her facial expression. I knew her answer before she said it. "No thanks. We don't need a ride."

Ouch. In other words, she didn't want a ride from *her mom*.

"Right. Well. We'll head off shortly. Enjoy your practice."

I said goodbye, and joined Jas in the walk-of-shame back to our place on the bench. As for Arianna, she had plunged back into the water, and was already halfway down the lane by the time we had settled back into our seats on the muggy pool deck.

"Well," Jas said, crossing legs and then her arms across her chest.

"Hmm." I rubbed the back of my neck, glad my hair was piled on top of my head and not lying heavily down my back. "Damn hot in here."

"Sure is." Jas looked wilted and it wasn't just the humidity. "Say Gill, do you have the number for that crazy therapist of yours somewhere? Maybe she'll have some crack ideas for me."

We burst out laughing, a masochistic cackle that was only acceptable between close friends. "No fair! You've got that sexy yoga guy. The crazy therapist is all mine."

"Fine. I'm damn well texting him within the next twenty-four hours."

"You do that! Because at least one of us needs some excitement."

We gathered our belongings and exited the sweltering pool deck, our middle-aged faces flushed with heat and whatever dignity we had left. Once outside, the brisk wind hit us with a gust of refreshing coolness.

"Want to grab lunch?" asked Jas.

I grimaced. "Wish I could. But I've got an errand to do..." and it would be better to just get it over with. If I had any intention of following through on Torres's homework, I would need to find some wench wear soon.

We hugged and said goodbye. Life was changing. Changing in ways we hadn't expected. Changing in ways we weren't quite ready for.

But we had each other.

Chapter Twelve

On my way over to the costume shop, I took a detour and hit up Starbucks for latte and banana bread. Given the sacrifice I was about to make for my marriage, I had no trouble justifying the comfort food.

I plugged the coordinates into my GPS and followed the directions to a semi-industrial part of town that I ventured to only when I took our empty beverage containers to the recycling depot.

When my GPS's voice – official and no-nonsense – announced, "Your destination is on the left," I obediently pulled into a strip-mall parking lot and assessed my surroundings.

The costume shop was tucked between a payday loans operation and a second-hand furniture store. It wasn't so much the neon sign that drew my eye; it was the mannequins in the front window. They were all dressed in a variety of fantasy garb. Leather jerkins, shiny chest plates, and jewel-encrusted swords hanging from leather-studded belts. Wait. Were those pointy ears on the far-left mannequin? Sticking out from under the felt Robin Hood–inspired hat? I squinted my eyes, trying to get a better look. Indeed, pointy they were. I took a sip of my latte for fortification.

Obviously, I had found the right place. Yet I hesitated in my car, slowly nursing my latte, just as any normal person would do. This was foolish. I should drive away. But the larp volunteer coordinator had suggested either this place or purchasing online, and I didn't have time left for an online purchase before my weekend of live-action hell.

I took a deep inhale and held it as long as possible. My

heart was hammering away, induced by a combination of stress and caffeine, no doubt. As the air escaped my lungs, I visualised the long list of educational credentials after Celeste Torres's name. She had to know what she was doing, didn't she?

Okay, Gill, get on with it. If you can't enter a somewhat-sketchy costume shop, how are you ever going to face an actual larp weekend? I could do this. Putting down my now-empty coffee cup, I got out of the car and made a beeline for the entrance before I could back down.

A shimmer of jingling bells, attached to the door chain above me, announced my arrival. I immediately looked towards the purchasing counter to say hello, but no one was there. In fact, I couldn't see anyone. Was the store open? Had the clerk stepped out for a coffee or forgotten to lock up for the weekend? Standing on the welcome mat – *Live Long and Prosper* in bright mustard letters – I took a quick survey of the shop.

My eyes were assaulted with a wide array of the unusual. All sorts of outfits were on display, many of which didn't look warm enough for medieval weekends stomping through the woods. Sexy nurse costumes, pirate getups, cave man outfits. It was as though an adult-themed version of Mr Dress-Up's tickle trunk had exploded, coating every surface of the small store in fantasy garb.

"Welcome." A honeyed voice coming from the back of the shop startled me. "Can I be of assistance?" Partly relieved I wouldn't need to make a second trip and partly frazzled that I was going to have to go through with this, I cleared my throat.

"Yes, hello?" I said, still trying to identify where the voice had originated.

From behind a rack of war hammers peeped what could only be described as a little old lady. She was tiny, probably not five feet tall, and was wearing a fuzzy sweater in a light pink hue. The sweater, unfortunately, clashed with her brilliant orange lipstick. I couldn't help but smile. Her round, cherubic face smiled back. The unease I'd felt since entering the parking lot dissipated. How could this possibly be intimidating?

"Oh, I hope so," I said. "I'm looking for a costume. For next weekend."

"Anything in particular, dear? I've got a few sale items over here...Racy Robin Hood, Naughty on the Nile, perhaps?" She pointed towards the far wall as her eyes gave my body the once over.

"Naughty on the what?" My hand automatically reached up and covered my heart as though I was about to have a heart attack. Who was the old lady now?

"On the Nile, dear. But perhaps something more literary. The Lady of Shallot? Hmmm?" She skirted around the war hammers and made her way over to me. Holding on to my elbow, she directed me to the women's section. It didn't take an expert to realise that some of the other store patrons had lifestyles a bit less traditional than my own.

"What did you say you needed this costume for, dear?" The old lady still had me by the elbow. She patted my arm as she continued to look me over in a professional way, assessing my frame for size and shape. "Professional or home use?"

Professional? Did she think I was...? Oh God!

"Oh! Um, actually, I'm headed out volunteering with this...group." I pulled open my purse and grabbed the email I'd printed out. "It's my very first time," I rushed on. "I'm not sure it's something I want to do on a regular basis. I'm just, you know, checking it out. Anyway, they directed me to your shop. They said I may be able to," I unfolded my note and read directly from the coordinator's email, "'rent a tavern wench tunic and accessories for the larp association member price seeing as you will be volunteering as an NPC.'" Oh God. I raced through that last part as my face flamed up.

"Oh, a non-player character! How exciting!" The shop assistant grinned up at me. Wow. She actually knew what all these acronyms were about. "Absolutely, dear. We can honour the membership price and just rent this time. I know it's a big commitment. And if you decide to make a more permanent investment, we would be most happy if you returned here for your follow-up purchase."

"Of course," I assured her. "Of course. I'm not sure it will be for me. But, ah, you never know. Besides," I added with my own smile, "you're probably the best supplier in town, from what I've been told." She was the kind of sweet senior a person wanted to please rather than offend.

This seemed to thrill her to no end, and it was now her turn to place her palm over her own heart. "That is so kind of you, dear. I do try. And tell you what, if you decide live action is for you, I'll take the rental price off the cost of your very own costume. Deal?"

"Deal."

As we headed to the checkout counter, she stopped at a bin of polished animal horns I hadn't noticed earlier.

"Can I interest you in a mead horn?" She swept her arm over the bin of animal body parts in a Vanna White–esque flourish. God knew what kind of animal they were originally from, and I tried my best to cover my aversion.

"They come in various sizes – good for more than just mead. They hold wine, water, even coffee. You can tie it to your waist with a leather strap so it's portable. Keep you hydrated on your journey, hmmm?"

"Right. I mean, no." I pictured tiny particles of powdered horn trapped in the tip of the vessel dislodging and ruining an otherwise good glass of wine. Whether the elderly lady was cute or not, I was not drinking out of that. "I'm allergic," I announced with a smile. Total lie, but the truth was not needed in every circumstance.

Fifteen minutes later, I was outside fumbling with my car keys, the proud tenant of my very own beige wench tunic, leather corset, and navy hooded over-cloak. I hid my costume in the trunk of my car. Holy shit. This was bizarre. But, I reminded myself, I was doing this for my marriage. In theory, at least. Either way, I was going to need something a little stronger than a latte, that was for damn sure.

Chapter Thirteen

It was late Friday afternoon, my stomach a rolling ball of anxiety as I stood on Jas's porch fumbling through my keychain for her house key. I kept a copy for emergencies and for holiday housesitting. Finding the right one, I unlocked and opened the door.

"Hello?" I called into the house. I didn't know if Arianna was home from school and didn't want to startle her. "It's just me."

I heard what sounded like cattle stomping down the stairs, and my beautiful goddaughter raced into sight.

"Arianna, honey!" I opened my arms and she hugged me back without hesitation. I felt a mix of bittersweet happiness as I kissed the top of her meticulously straightened and product-infused locks. I didn't take these moments for granted; I knew from my own youth that not all fourteen-year-olds were so free with their affection. But then again, I wasn't the woman who had to set the rules or enforce them. I briefly contemplated asking about the unknown boy from her grandfather's birthday, but just as quickly, I put the idea aside. I had no idea what to say anyway.

"Mom says you're surprising Ralph or something?"

Slipping off my flats, I followed her into the kitchen. "Something like that. It's kind of a silly idea, really. And," I raised my hands and spread my fingers in the universal sign that meant *Stop, this is serious*, "it's completely secret, okay?"

Arianna nodded. "'Kay."

"You can't tell anyone. Ever."

"That's cool." Arianna was looking curiously at my bags for possible clues. I had the shopping bag from the costume shop and a hairbrush, makeup bag, hair dryer, pyjamas, and wool socks all spilling haphazardly from my duffle bag. I'd left my sleeping bag at the front door. I had gathered my stuff in the morning before going to work, and I hoped I hadn't forgotten anything I would need.

"So…do you need anything?" she asked.

"Just a place to change and get organised. Ralph's at home still and I don't want to…wreck his surprise." I grimaced.

"Maybe Mom's room?" Arianna suggested before leading the way upstairs in that fast stomp that only the young could do. I smiled as I followed in a considerably more sedate fashion. Although she was on the verge of adulthood, Arianna still moved with the excitement of youth. I had known her, and loved her, since the day she had been born, and to me she was perfect.

Arianna flipped the lights on in her mother's room and flopped down on the bed.

"I've got it from here," I said. "If you have something better to do, no worries." Placing my bags down, I hoped she would take the hint. I was pretty certain I didn't want an audience. Besides, I could see one question leading to another, and putting some connection back into the old marriage wasn't exactly a topic I wanted to explore with her.

But no luck. Arianna pulled the leather corset out of the shopping bag before I could stop her. "Whoa!"

Great. Humiliation would be starting very early.

Arianna was looking from me to the corset and back again. "What kind of surprise is this, anyhow?"

My cheeks flushed. "Nothing quite as exciting as you may be thinking!" I sat down beside her and tried to get the garment back as I chose my words with care. She evaded me and started posing with the corset in front of the floor-length mirror Jas had in the corner of her room.

"Okay. So, Ralph is into this kind of game. It's like a…a board game, but you act it out."

"Clue!"

80

"You act it out in the woods."

"Clue in the Forest!"

"Well...I guess, but it's not really a mystery, I don't think. But maybe. Anyway, the people dress up in medieval clothes rather than stuffy British suits."

"And you're the sexy lady-in-waiting!" She was bouncing on the edge of the bed in excitement and hadn't yet stopped to question the idiocy of the game itself.

"Um, well, more like the kitchen help. I'm going as a volunteer. To help out, you know? These, um, people – or players – act out this game all weekend. And part of the game is, well, you have to stay in the story's character the whole time. So even the food and sleeping quarters and everything are supposed to be old-fashioned." I had now practically exhausted my entire novice larp knowledge bank.

"That's pretty cool." Arianna was still holding the corset against her body, turning from side to side while scrutinizing her reflection in the mirror.

"Um. Yes. Cool, I guess. A bit different, but you know, I'm checking it out and," I searched my memory for Dr Torres's words, "I'm being supportive of Ralph's hobby-thing."

"Can I come?" she asked.

"Er...I think you have to be eighteen." My immediate reaction was surprise. Didn't Arianna realise larp was not cool? Calling it unusual was about the nicest thing I could say about it. But as I watched her continue to pose with the corset in the mirror, I flashed to my own youth. When I was close to her age, I couldn't understand why my parents were hung up on people being gay; I'd always prided myself on being more open-minded than my elders. And now look at me. Not quite forty, and I had trouble accepting my husband's hobby. Maybe Arianna was right. Maybe this whole larp thing wasn't such a big deal.

"But I'll ask around when I'm there. See if they do any all-ages events, okay?"

"Great! Can I get one of these?" She held up the leather

corset, and I choked on my attempt at open-mindedness.

"Nope, I highly doubt it. Not that it wouldn't look great on you, but your mother'd kill me!" I took the garment back and dug out the rest of the rented costume from the shopping bag. It was time to get on with it.

I walked into Jas's ensuite and closed the door firmly behind me. If I was really going to do this, the transformation could at least happen with some semblance of privacy. I folded my own clothes into a neat pile before giving the beige homespun tunic-style dress a good shake in an attempt to knock the creases out of it. Here we go, I thought.

I scrunched it on over my head, the fabric cascading down to my toes. I'd be lucky not to trip. The sleeves were long, coming over my wrist and ending in a point on the back of my hand. Was this going to be safe over an open fire?

Something was wrong with the neckline of the dress. It was gaping, and I suddenly realised it was meant to sit off the shoulder. Oh great. Were kitchen wenches immune to the cold, or were they just okay with freezing? I turned my attention to the leather corset that went on top of the tunic. It had wide shoulder straps that covered my own bra straps (no way was I taking that off; there were limits to this roleplaying, and I was not walking around all weekend freezing myself in this off-the-shoulder dress with my nipples performing their own live-action show). The bottom of the corset sat just above my pubic bone and flared out over my hips. I took the laces in each hand and tightened them a little before tying a bow. Tight enough to give me a little bit of a waist but loose enough I could still breathe.

Bang, bang. Arianna was already rapping on the bathroom door. "Are you about done in there? Come on out!"

There was no way I wanted to leave the bathroom. But if I couldn't face my godchild in wench gear – a person who loved me unconditionally – then how the heck would I face Ralph and a bunch of strangers?

Here goes nothing. I sucked in my gut, slid the bathroom door open, and took one step into the bedroom.

"Okay, don't laugh."

Arianna sat back on the bed and gave me the once over.

"Well?" I said. This was terrible. No grown woman should be subjected to this kind of scrutiny – ever. "Just tell me. Do I look completely ridiculous or what?"

"You look...you look..."

I couldn't tell what she was thinking from her expression.

"Totally hot, Auntie!"

"Seriously? Do you think so?"

"Ya!"

She was bouncing up and down on the edge of the bed, her hands clasped together. Yes, I loved this kid. No one, in my entire memory, had ever bounced up and down, hands clasped together, and told me I was hot. I smiled in gratitude, then shuffled over to stand in front of the full-length mirror.

"Like, just look at your boobs!"

"Arianna!" My hands flew up and covered the top of my middle-aged breasts, which were being pushed up over the top of my corset. This thing worked better than a twenty-first-century miracle bra. I turned to the side. It was an all-over miracle garment, really. My tummy was completely obliterated by the sheer strength of the leather and laces.

"Wow, perhaps medieval wenches knew what they were doing." I turned around and looked over my shoulder to check out my rear end. Not bad. Not bad at all.

I grinned at Arianna. "I couldn't have done this without you, honey. Thanks for your support! I was worried, but I think I can do this! I totally owe you."

"How about you buy me one of those leather things for Christmas, then?"

"Sure. In five years!" I laughed, then started to pack up the haphazard mess I'd brought with me into some semblance of duffle organization when we heard the front door open.

"Hello?" called Jas.

"We're up here," Arianna bellowed. "Come check out your hot friend!"

"Don't laugh," I called down just as quickly.

Jas made her way up to the transformation studio, also known as her bedroom, and opened the door. She took one look at me, and her perfectly manicured eyebrows shot up under her bangs. But thankfully, she didn't laugh. I twirled to give her the full effect.

"So," she said. "You're really doing this?"

"I am. The volunteering kitchen part, at least. We'll see how that part goes." I glanced over at Arianna, hoping Jas would pick up my hint that I didn't want to discuss everything with her daughter present.

"And Gill said I can go some other time," said Arianna.

"After I check it out and see what it's all about."

Arianna flopped back on the bed, her head landing on the pillow. "I think it will be a lot more awesome than hanging out here all weekend."

I watched as my friend immediately took the bait. Folding her arms across her chest, Jas leaned against the door frame. "Certainly more awesome than that mystery boy you refuse to tell me about."

Arianna didn't bother responding. The energy in the room had slid from fun to confrontational, and I was inept at changing it.

"Well, okay, ladies, thanks for your help. I think I'm ready to go. Ready to jump into my time machine and go serve some hungry warriors meat and ale. Wish me…luck!"

I said goodbye to Arianna and then Jas walked me downstairs and out to my car.

"Good luck, Gill," Jas said, hugging me in farewell. "Honestly, this takes a lot of courage. Regardless of what I said before, I'm not sure a lot of people could do this for their spouse."

I felt a flash of guilt. Was I doing this for Ralph or was it really because I wanted to prove how unreasonable his priorities were?

"I'm actually scared shitless!" I confided.

"Maybe think of it as an adventure. You cook a little meat. Cut some veggies. Check out some men in beards and pointy ears. Potentially spice up your marriage…or get the answers you need. Besides, Arianna's right: you look damn hot, so what's to lose?"

My marriage, I thought. And more than likely, she was thinking it too. But neither of us said it aloud. "My dignity," I settled on instead. "This is larping we're talking about, after all. But it's too late to back out now. The kitchen is counting on me."

"That's the spirit," Jas encouraged. I got into the car and firmly shut the door.

I was on my way.

Chapter Fourteen

Finding the Fisher Creek campsite wasn't difficult. The volunteer organiser had been only too happy to send me her new-recruit map. It was a bird's eye view of the encampment site, complete with details such as parking, latrines (What? Uncool!), sleeping quarters for volunteers, the kitchen mess, and the gaming boundaries for the live-action participants.

And even without the map, I wouldn't have had trouble locating it; I'd been there before. Ralph and I had pitched our tent at this campground a time or two when we used to explore Kananaskis and the Rocky Mountains on a regular basis. Whether we were scrambling up steep shale inclines or meandering trails through wooded glades, hiking had been one of the activities we loved about our new home in Alberta.

We'd read every guide book we could get our hands on. With every new trail we'd tackled, we'd been convinced that this time we would encounter a bear. And so we'd taken precautions. We carried bear spray, strapped to our waist and easily accessible. We wore ridiculous little bells that would jingle as we hiked up trails, notifying wild animals of our approach – until more experienced hikers informed us the bells weren't worth squat.

We had a routine. We'd drive out and set up our tent as early as we could on Friday night and then be out all day Saturday on some trail or other, only to return tired, exhausted, and completely happy. Sunday morning we'd sleep in, the tent slowly heating up in the sunshine – or not. Sometimes the ping of rain or splat of wet snow fell on the tent fly, and we'd cuddle together, make love, and barter over who would actually get up and get the fire going.

We admired the families hiking on the trails, and daydreamed together about how we'd continue camping after our own children were born. We discussed the extra equipment we'd need, carrier backpacks and portable cots and which brands offered the best value.

On all those countless hikes, we'd never seen a bear. The bear spray had expired and hit the trash. And the extra equipment? It hadn't needed purchasing.

Today a few dozen cars were parked alongside the highway near the campground entrance. Right. No modern technology inside the playing area. The coordinator had been firm: no cars, no cellphones, no twenty-first-century reminders. I parked behind a black F150, which partially hid my car from the road. No need to advertise my presence until I was ready to do so. Looking around, I did not see Ralph's vehicle, and I wasn't surprised. It would probably take him longer to get here as he worked right till five most days.

Grabbing my sleeping gear and nondescript duffle bag from the trunk (along with the warning about no technology, I'd also been informed that logos were seriously frowned upon), I took one last moment to steel myself. *Okay, here goes nothing.*

Trying my best to reduce my nervous energy, I focused on the trees, on the wind rippling through their spring leaves and on the white bark of the aspens as they stretched to the sky. I passed through the entrance and into the campground, and despite my nerves, I couldn't help but breathe deeply. It was beautiful out here.

I looked around. At first glance it didn't appear much had changed: same curved road down the hill, and in the valley a scattering of trees and numbered campsites, each with their own metal fire-pit. See? No big deal. Except the groups of weekend campers and hikers had been exchanged for colourful marquee-style tents that looked, to my admittedly untrained eye, more Disney than authentic. I could see small groupings of people already wandering around in brown tunics or macho leather-studded armour. Some people had even stained their skin green and were sporting the pointy ears I'd seen on the costume shop mannequin. Okay, so much for nature-induced tranquillity. I gulped down my apprehension. It wasn't as if I hadn't known I'd be out of my element.

Maybe it would be okay to spend the entire weekend getting drunk on spiced rum in the kitchen? Or at least a little bit tipsy, just to take the edge off. Because how else was I going to look at these people with a straight face? I could've kicked myself for not buying one of the pretentious skull flasks at the costume shop. I could've stuffed it down my bodice.

Sticking to the outskirts of the crowd, I stopped to unscrunch my map, which had somehow become balled up in my sweaty hand. Where was I? The map didn't make sense. It seemed as though I should be near the kitchen area, but there were no buildings in sight. I looked at the sun, trying to figure out which way was north. Who bloody knew where north was, anyway?

During our phone conversation, the volunteer organiser had stressed that everyone needed to stay in character, at all times, all weekend, unless in an OOP area. I'd had to ask for clarification on OOP. It meant out of play.

Both the volunteers' sleep quarters and the kitchen were OOP, for player characters, or PCs. Those were the people, like Ralph, who were here to play the game. PCs were not allowed to enter OOP areas except during meal times, and that was confined to the kitchen area.

What I needed to find was this OOP area. Turning the map around in my hands, I realised I might actually be right in the heart of the live-action area for players. Or maybe not.

Right. It was not likely I'd figure out the damn map. That left me with two choices: I could either wander about hoping to find my destination by chance, or I could ask someone for directions. Getting to the OOP area sooner rather than later seemed a good idea, and that meant approaching someone for help. Looking around, my immediate choices included a pack of men with beards, armour, and fake swords, who were currently playing a game with rocks on a picnic table (Rocks? Come on!); a group of green people with pointy ears, their heads close together and whispering to each other; and an attractive-looking woman with fairy wings strapped to her back, butterflies somehow attached to her eyebrows, a plunging neckline, and a quiver of felt-tipped arrows in her hand.

I decided on the green people. They didn't have any weapons. I approached the group, ready to explain my predicament.

"Um, hi there," I said. They simultaneously turned and stared at me, the whites of their unblinking eyes looking spookily bright next to their Kermit skin. As no one reached out to shake my extended hand, I awkwardly let it drop. "I was just wondering if you could direct me to the—"

"Peep, bleep," hissed the green man closest to me. *Um?* I looked around at the other members of the green group, but everyone was still staring as though it was me who had done something odd. I took a step back.

The green guy who'd addressed me took two quick shuffles towards me and made an alarming "Bleep, shreek!" in my face.

"Oh my God." The words whipped out of me as I hyperventilated. A green woman shuffled forward and placed her fingertips on my neck.

I held up my sleeping bag and duffle bag as a shield in front of me and knocked her fingers off my neck. The rest of the greenies immediately started to swarm, reaching out and touching my clothing and hair. What was I supposed to do? Other than scream? I looked back up the hill I had just walked down. Could I make it back to the security of my car in a long-ass dress before these green guys did...who knows what to me?

Think, Campbell. Think. The green guys had made a tight circle around me. They'd stopped touching my body, and now their arms were entwined as their bodies gyrated to the sound of their bleep, bleeps. What the bleeping shit was going on, anyway?

Was this what the volunteer coordinator had meant by staying in character, or were these guys some kind of LSD junkies disguised as part of the larp community? What kind of things go on at these events, anyway? *Come on, Gill.* I took a breath. I'd just have to try again.

"So, I'm looking for...the, um, kitchen area. Could you, er, point me in the right direction?" I could feel my face flaming because I had fallen into my standard habit – speaking super loud, super slow – when talking to someone who didn't speak fluent English. But seriously, these people probably grocery shopped at the same store I did and had excellent English. They were just choosing not to use it. Unless they were really LSD junkies and had completely fried their brainstems. The gyrating was starting to pick up speed, the circle closing in around me more and more tightly, and the bleeping was now a hissing taunt.

"Hi there, little lady," a deep voice boomed.

Oh shit. What now? I turned around. One of the sword-carrying manly types had edged up behind the group and stood threateningly close to the green orb circling me. He caressed the hilt of his fake sword in a decidedly suggestive fashion. Good Lord. From the pot to the fire. But it worked. The green people backed away from him, clearly not wanting an altercation.

"I couldn't help but overhear you were looking for the kitchens." He reached into the circle of green bodies, grabbed my elbow, and pulled me out. The green people twittered and gabbled but did nothing to try to pull me back.

"I can see you are new here, so let me give you a hint. A beautiful lady like you shouldn't be interacting with elfish scum. And certainly not if you were my female." He gave me some kind of knowing male look and peered down at my corset-enhanced chest. I clutched the edges of my hooded cape together. Was this really happening? In a haze, I allowed him to place my hand on his forearm and steer me away, presumably in the direction of the kitchens.

"I am Ivan, the Great Wanderer. Leader of this troupe." He used his free hand to refer to the four lads and the one tough-looking broad who were accompanying us. Along with a variety of hatchets, knives, and spears, each carried a matching shield picturing two wolves biting each other's tail. The wolves formed a ring about each of the much-dented and hammered-upon shields and looked to be hand painted. I couldn't fathom how much time might have been spent crafting the devices, all for a weekend hobby. But now was not the time to ask.

"Nice to meet you, Ivan. I," and here I used my hand to touch my own chest importantly, "am Gretchen, the Great... Wenchen." *What the...?* Had that just come out of my mouth? Indeed it had. But who cared? It was just nuts anyway. "I am here to, er, assist with food for the weekend. My first time. Just checking things out. I do thank you for your help."

Ivan graciously insisted on carrying my bags. I didn't bother pulling out my useless map, which I'd shoved into my pocket during my elfish detainment, and instead trusted my rescuer not to lead me astray. His friends, er, *troupe*, fanned out and watched the trees around us – for what or who, God only knew.

For once, it was nice to meet the kind of guy who could carry a whole conversation himself. He talked about his great and powerful broadsword – it sounded more to me like he was talking about the merits of his manhood, but I kept it professional. Which means I did not snigger or make any jokes. My recent experience had highlighted the fact that I was obviously the minority here.

I was only an hour from the city limits, but I'd never experienced anything like this in my life. It felt like waking up in a foreign country. Did Ralph accost helpless kitchen maids? I hoped not. So far, this had been an odder experience than I'd anticipated, and that was saying something.

As we rounded one last stand of trees, I could also see a cabin and cooking shack, in front of which a few cooking fires were already burning. Needless to say, I'd never been so thankful to see a black cauldron hanging over a smouldering fire.

"Thanks for your assistance, kind sir." I took my belongings back from Ivan and scampered off as fast as my thirty-eight-year-old legs in floor-length homespun would let me.

"I'm not a *sir*, milady, I'm a scoundrel," he called after my departing backside. His troupe laughed as I entered the OOP area, and I'd no doubt my face was a flaming mask of mortification.

Chapter Fifteen

After a quick orientation from Margaret, a seasoned larp volunteer, I set my belongings on one of the bottom bunks in the volunteer dorm. The cabin I'd seen from the path contained our sleeping quarters and a basic bathroom for volunteer use. As we weren't technically players, we would have heat, electricity, and flush toilets. I was not complaining. The June nights were still brisk, and I had a fleeting thought of Ralph sleeping on the hard ground in one of the dramatic tents I had seen earlier. But it was his choice, and he obviously didn't mind.

I was assigned to washing dishes. As it was Friday night and everyone was arriving at different times, the meal had apparently been prepared ahead of time (quite a lovely beef stew, actually; volunteers were presently scooping it out of crockpots and filling the cooking pots hanging over the smouldering camp fire outside...because that was authentic). Players came and went, gathering food and eating in a slow trickle. The dirty dishes entered the kitchen in the same unhurried way. I didn't mind. The repetitive chore helped to soothe my adrenaline rush and frazzled nerves.

The dishes, referred to as *trenchers*, were flat squares of either wood or metal, and of the latter, I seriously questioned lead content. Cutlery was limited to hand-carved wooden spoons. The player characters, PCs, were expected to bring their own personal eating knives to cut meat. Thankfully, a stack of plastic cutlery was available for volunteer use, although I noticed some of the NPCs with more elaborate costumes had their own era-inspired utensils.

From the dishwashing station, I could hardly see the player eating area through the open doorway, and I relaxed knowing that it was unlikely I'd come face to face with Ralph. For the next hour or two, that is. On the other hand, it did provide me an opportunity to expand upon my paltry larp knowledge base. Perhaps it was my rattled appearance or wide-eyed expression, but Margaret seemed to be going out of her way to ease me into the larp environment. She introduced me to other volunteers and stopped by periodically to help dry dishes. It was during one of these times that she managed to corner me into divulging personal information.

"So...what brings you out to larp? You're a first-timer, I assume?"

I handed her a sopping wet piece of wood that had served as someone's dinner plate, trying to buy time as I formed an answer. "You've got that right...I'm a virgin larper."

"I can probably guess at the answer to my next question, then. As you're not *In Game*, I'm going to assume that either your spouse is a larper or you're looking for a spouse. Am I right?"

I had to smile. "Are you telling me there are only two reasons to be out here?" I managed to avoid answering directly; if I said my husband was out here, she might wonder why he didn't come to the kitchen and check on me. And if I said I was looking for someone – well, that could get awkward fast, if my experience with Ivan the Wandering Romeo had taught me anything.

"There's another motivation that draws people to the larp kitchens...but you don't look like a sociology student digging for research."

"You're kidding." I choked back laughter. "That happens?"

"Sure, occasionally. I like to play it up for them; it's fun freaking them out." Margaret winked at me, and I handed her a wooden bowl to dry before asking her a question.

"So, Margaret, assuming you're also not a sociology

student, I can then only assume you're on the hunt for a husband or are perhaps supporting your own husband in his quest for larp adventure."

She laughed. "I think I'm a bit too old to be attracting men folk in this get up." She was also wearing a floor-length tunic, but in a soft grey and minus the leather corset. I guessed her age to be late fifties, and her frame was heavier in a very comfortable way. I had gravitated to her instantly because of her grandmotherly look. But I supposed men seeking women might not gravitate the same way. "Mike – that's my husband – and I are pretty much regulars at these events. We've even gone on larp vacations – The Battle of Hastings and…. Have you heard of the Duchy of Bicolline?"

The ducky of what? I shook my head, reasonably sure I'd never heard of it and was unlikely to add it to my bucket list.

"It's this permanent medieval town they've built in Quebec. They host a seven-day larp event, and we've travelled out to it a few times. It's near Shawinigan."

I'd never heard of Shawinigan either. But I was curious about Margaret's enthusiasm. I'd never met any larp wives before.

"So," I began carefully, "is it Mike who's into larp, or both of you?"

"Both of us, actually. I used to participate in game play, but now I prefer hanging out with the other women. Besides, it's nice not twisting my ankles in gopher holes with a shrieking banshee chasing after you, you know what I mean?"

She jabbed her elbow lightly into my ribs. I handed her the last metal trencher to dry and smiled. "Gotta hate those banshees," I said, laughing weakly.

"So? Are you going to tell me? Spousal support or on the prowl?"

"Spousal support." I turned my back and emptied the water from the sink. I needed to change the conversation fast before she asked who my husband was. "What do we do now?"

"Now we sit around. Drink some tea by the fire. Watch the players rush back and forth and heckle them if required. You should join us."

I glanced around the kitchen, filled with strangers chatting and completing chores and appearing entirely normal despite the costumes. There must be at least a few other kindred souls who thought this whole thing was a giant waste of time and who were completely annoyed to be a lesser priority than a moronic game. Or, at the least, comfortable souls like Margaret, who was surprisingly easy to be around.

"All right," I agreed. "I'll be right out." Not only would I have a chance to do some spying in the open while being camouflaged within a group, I would also be chipping away at Torres's homework. Baby steps. The larp version of mini-golf.

Chapter Sixteen

After gathering my hooded cape off my bunk, I joined the rest of the kitchen crew outdoors. The metal brackets used to hold the cauldrons over the fire had been removed, leaving a traditional twenty-first-century blackened metal fire-pit with flip-up grate. Although the night had already cooled considerably, the fire had been built up, and the bright orange flames and the smell of camping smoke were welcoming.

Instead of lawn chairs, the volunteers sat on wooden benches and tree stumps. My rear-end was going to miss the soft comfort of woven plastics, but I took a seat on a wooden bench beside Margaret.

I didn't know the time, but I thought it must be late. Being early June and this far north, I knew it would be nearly 11 p.m. before the sky had darkened enough to affect our vision. As it was, I could still distinguish many of the players' faces as they travelled along the path I'd taken earlier in the day.

As for the volunteers, most were sitting around the fire, chatting in groups of two and three. Many seemed to know each other. I listened as they discussed children, the weather forecast for the weekend, the harried drive up, and recent current events. Other than an intense amount of homespun, it seemed no different from any other campfire gathering of women.

I did my best to participate in the small talk but was happy to listen more than contribute. In truth, I was exhausted and looking forward to my bunk bed, as sketchy as it may be. (Because honestly, what camp bed wasn't sketchy? Moulds, bugs, and past users and their unknown habits – it was best not to think about it too much.)

I was emotionally drained from the week of planning, and now that I was actually here, the anxiety and adrenaline had washed away. The realization that the other volunteers were really quite normal people had helped.

Out of habit, I lifted my wrist to check the time. Of course, my watch wasn't there. I had "discarded the trappings of modern industry," as instructed. It now sat in the bottom of my duffle bag with my powered-off cellphone.

"Would you like some wine?" A young woman carrying a carafe of glazed clay in one hand and a stack of wooden tumblers in the other had stopped in front of me.

"Yes, definitely." Was there any chance I'd say no? She poured a cup of red wine for me and for Margaret before moving on to the next bench.

"Margaret, where on earth did they get all these rustic supplies?" I took a moment to appreciate my wooden goblet, inwardly happy I hadn't been handed one of the mead horns I'd seen in the costume shop.

"Oh, all kinds of places: garage sales, websites selling larp gear – even church bazaars. That goblet you have looks like it came from some Easter play production, if you ask me."

A small ripple of guilt washed over me as I thought of Ralph's business idea, which I'd shot down so quickly. But weren't all these props evidence that there were already plenty of suppliers of larp gear? I'd probably been right all along even though I hadn't known anything about it. Although…he'd been talking specifically about weapons, hadn't he? It was hard remembering the details now, I'd been that angry.…

The rapid pounding of soft-soled shoes on the pathway drew my attention. A group of players clothed like peasants were running helter-skelter past our group. They were in such a rush, they did not spare us even a glance as they raced by.

But in any case, it was too late. A second group in black

robes were closing in. Within seconds, they were throwing what looked like beanbags (For the love of God, what was this, elementary school?) hand over fist at the hunted group. It was happening so fast, I could hardly tell if any of the bags made contact, but some must have. Because first one, then two more peasants hit the ground and lay as if dead. Or stunned. Or...or something.

The light from the fire threw the remaining players' shadows into long eerie relief as the black-robed players began to congratulate each other with whoops and slaps on the back. Not one of them turned to look towards the fire. But, I supposed, we NPCs were as much props as the trenchers or the wooden goblet in my hands.

"What on earth?" I finally managed to ask.

"The cloth bags are magic," Margaret said.

I turned away from the scene to look at her. "Magic?"

"That's right, magic. Larp only works if every player follows the rules for the fantasy world they are playing within. They've got to stay in character and follow the storyline, no matter how imaginative, or it just doesn't work. If they didn't, it'd be like halfway through a baseball game a player deciding that they'll go directly to second base and skip first. It doesn't work. Ruins it for everyone."

"So...if someone hits you with a beanbag and they say it's magic, you need to fall down as though it were?"

"Exactly." Margaret grinned and winked at me before taking a sip of her wine. I took a decent sip of my own wine, finishing my glass. I had a flashback to the larp video I'd watched from the safety of my kitchen. I wondered why the players tonight hadn't said anything like "magic bag three, magic bag three," but I really didn't care enough to ask.

More wine might be a good idea. To take the edge off. I was looking around the circle for the woman who'd brought the jug around earlier when I heard it. Again the sound of running, but this time it was coming through the underbrush and trees behind us.

Squinting my eyes, I couldn't see anything moving. Not

only had the sun finally set, but I was also looking from the brightness of the campfire into the darkness of the woods. I quickly turned my head back towards the magic people in black robes. Couldn't they hear it? Someone was approaching.

But the magic bag throwers were either unconcerned or still caught up in their victory. They were taking their sweet time searching for missing beanbags around the fallen victims and their fortune ran out.

The volunteers had all stopped talking now and their attention had switched to a red-caped, lone archer. Standing just outside the ring of firelight, she took a long bow off her shoulder and notched an arrow.

Really? An arrow? Wasn't that lethal? I leaned towards Margaret and whispered, "Isn't that, like, seriously dangerous?"

"The arrow's rubber tipped. It'll just leave a bruise. The archer will be aiming for the kill zone."

"Kill zone?"

"It's part of the rules. You can only hit certain parts of the body with weapons."

The archer took aim at one of the magic guys who was busy tucking beanbags into a fur pouch attached to his belt. As the archer continued to draw the bowstring back, I suddenly caught a glimpse of her face. My hand clenched my empty goblet in shock.

Lauren. The flutist from the orchestra. My freaking colleague. There must be at least a hundred people out here, and I had to cross paths with her on the first night? Just my luck.

I lifted my wine glass to shield my face from the firelight, but it wasn't needed. Just like the earlier players, Lauren didn't spare a glance in the NPCs' direction.

Lauren let loose her bow, and instantly the arrow crossed the clearing and hit her prey in the shoulder. The magic man yelped in pain and surprise, alerting his companions to Lauren's presence, before falling to the dirt. His friends left him and ran off. Random beanbags were haphazardly thrown over their shoulders in their haste to leave the archer's range and prevent her following.

The kitchen crew had remained silent through the scene, but now they broke out into whoops and catcalls directed at the retreating magic men. Meanwhile Lauren had approached the remaining players, both peasant and magical, who still languished on the ground. She took something small out of her pocket and distributed whatever it was to each of the peasants on the ground. She then took off one of the emblems on the magic guy's own wrist.

"She's taking one of his health chips away and giving some life to the others. See?"

I did see. The players on the ground got up, dusted themselves off, and started walking away as though nothing had happened. And, in fact, nothing had.

Or had it? Because now I had two people to evade. If I could barely explain to myself why I was here, and I'd yet to reveal my presence to Ralph, then the only thing running into Lauren would do was complicate the situation.

That night I lay in my bunk bed, sleepless. I usually had trouble sleeping anywhere new, and this was certainly new. I was glad for my own sleeping bag, and I was definitely glad I wasn't on the hard earth in a tent. A pillow would have been nice. Instead, my head rested on my folded cloak, and that was "roughing it" enough for me. Something told me I wouldn't be using my straightener in the morning.

Trying to ignore the random snoring of other volunteers on the bunks surrounding me, I focused on the noises outside the cabin. It sounded like any other camping weekend and was comforting. Muffled voices in conversation around some campfire carried on the night air. The occasional hoot of an owl out hunting. Later, the howling of coyotes enjoying a midnight romp through a neighbouring field; probably kilometres away, but in the night their laughing barks sounded much closer.

I had a sudden urge to text Ralph. To reach out and connect with him in some way, if only to get a clue to where in the camp he was. But even if I could sneak my phone out of my duffle bag, he wouldn't have his. It was against the rules to have any modern technology at a larp. And anyway, even when I sent a text to Ralph in the city, he was the king of the one-word response:

How's your day going?

Good.

Could you pick up some laundry soap on the way home?

Sure.

What should we have for dinner?

Whatever.

What, Ralph, is the goddamn point in being married when you aren't ever around when I need you?

Jeez, Gill. Enough.

Okay. So it was possible to get a three-word reply.

I rolled over, trying to get comfortable but managing only to get more tied up in my sleeping bag. Sleep was not coming to me. Instead, my mind wandered back to my rescue earlier in the evening. My knight in costume armour, who had liberated me from the elves and guided me to the safety of the kitchens. He hadn't exactly been Mel Gibson in *Braveheart*.

But it had been a long time since a man had noticed me. Or had gone out of his way to be gallant towards me. It had felt nice. In a youthful sort of way. It had left me feeling a little giddy and self-conscious, but flattered.

Some guy who went by the name Ivan the Wanderer had checked out my middle-aged breasts today. How weird was that? But, still, it'd been a long time. I blushed all alone in the dark. To be fair, I didn't usually go around wearing a leather corset. Perhaps I should. I smiled to myself. Arianna would get a kick out of that.

It looked like Jas was definitely moving towards dating. I wondered what it would be like, having men notice you. And imagine letting them know you noticed them back! It was hard not to feel dating was a lot more exciting than marriage. Energising. Freeing. I missed that.

And I was only in my late thirties. I had decades left with Ralph. Would they all feel so humdrum? So void of excitement? But if I left, could I really trade in the security and stability of marriage for feeling completely alive and desired? Was there any way those two things could be compatible, or, as I feared, were they truly mutually exclusive?

But that's why you are here, I reminded myself, to see what you can do about the dwindling marriage connection. I felt a little twinge, and it wasn't the sleeping bag zipper. It was the guilt that had accompanied me all week.

Torres hadn't meant for me to use larp as a way to spy on Ralph. I was supposed to be showing Ralph that I could be open to his interests and that quality time with him was important enough to me that I'd make sacrifices (like sleeping in a sketchy bunk bed; there was probably a spider hanging just inches above my face, and I couldn't even see it in the dark).

Maybe I should have been honest with Ralph. Let him know I was coming to check larp out, to be part of what he was interested in. Would he have been happy? Would he have gallantly shown me around the camp? Maybe. I could imagine him giving me the campground tour, but Ralph flirting with me like Ivan had? His ill-tempered and needy wife? Not likely.

And what if I'd told him I was coming out and he'd said no, don't come? What if he didn't want me here at all? Larp was his thing; his time to do what he wanted to do without his cantankerous wife vacillating between cold rejection and angry retorts.

And maybe this was his time to do what my guide had done – flirt with other women while under cover. Maybe he felt he had more in common with someone who was into larp than with someone he had lived with for fifteen long years. After all this time, it didn't seem we had a lot connecting us. Other than the electricity bill. The mortgage. The *married* box we checked on the annual civic census.

I shivered inside my sleeping bag and tried to wiggle down further. The coyotes were again cackling in the distance, seemingly in pleasure of my misery. I closed my eyes and did the only thing that seemed to come naturally: my *ujjayi* breath from yoga. Inhaling and exhaling through my nose, I pictured my anxiety leaving my body with each exhale. But unlike in a yoga class, this time my breathing combined with another practice learned much earlier in life. Likely in the basement classroom with a Sunday school teacher I'd long forgotten.

With each inhale, I questioned God. Was there any purpose to marriage? Was there any hope that Ralph and I could be happy with each other after all these years? Because there would be no distractions. No children to bind us. No future grandchildren to glue us together.

It was just Ralph and I. And right now, that didn't seem enough.

Chapter Seventeen

I woke with a start. Had I heard something?

Through the cabin window, I could see the heavy darkness of night had lifted, revealing the early morning dawn. I yawned and lifted my left arm out from my sleeping bag only to once again stare at my naked wrist. Oh yes, no watch. This was 1408 or whatever era existed before people concerned themselves with wristwatch accountability.

There it was again. The sound that had awoken me. No way. Was that really an ever-loving rooster? Lying on my back, I rolled my eyes. *You've got to be kidding me.* When Margaret had mentioned getting up when the rooster crowed, I'd assumed it was an expression. But sure enough, the other volunteers had begun to stretch and move around in their individual bunks.

An ordinary Saturday morning flashed through my mind. Sleep till 10 a.m. Wake up to coffee. Read a book. Maybe go for a walk or get caught up on some music practice. I might even wear pyjamas till half past noon.

It did not involve serving breakfast to hordes of men and women in face paint.

I rolled to my side, my thoughts shifting to Ralph. If I had ever needed proof that some small part of me thought my marriage was worth fighting for, here it was. There was simply no other explanation for what the hell I was doing. I smiled to myself; I had certainly woken up more positive than I'd been the previous night.

I got dressed in the freezing bathroom, brushed my teeth, attempted to calm my frizzy hair into some semblance of normal, and gave up. Instead I resorted to my haphazard bun, and then applied the must-haves – face cream with a heavy dose of SPF to keep the freckle population in control and mascara to help define my eyes. Alas, there was nothing left to do but head to the kitchen and start helping with breakfast.

"You're on oatmeal, Gillian." Margaret pointed outside, where the cauldrons had already been hung on their brackets. Flames were licking at the bottom of the blackened pots, and I had flashbacks of watching old Macbeth films in high school English.

"Sounds good. Any chance of grabbing a coffee?"

"Sure is. If these PCs expect a warm brekkie, then my volunteers can certainly grab a coffee." She handed me a pewter beer stein. It was heavy, but it would hold liquid, and I certainly wasn't complaining.

I made my way outside with steaming coffee, a hand-carved wooden spoon, and my cloak fastened under my chin. I was thankful for the leggings I had packed as well as the wool sweater layered over my leather corset but under my cloak. The morning was chilly, even when standing next to a fire.

One of the other volunteers measured out the oatmeal, water, butter, and salt, placing the lot into my cauldron. My job was to keep stirring the porridge as it cooked to prevent it from congealing or burning to the bottom of the pot.

A table was set up near the cooking fire, and large stacks of rustic bowls and spoons were brought out. Margaret was overseeing the set up and seemed to be the one who knew what was going on.

"How's that porridge coming along?" She came over and looked into my cauldron.

I lifted my wooden spoon and let the mush drip off in large globs. The oats looked as though they had softened. "Looks almost done to me."

"Good. The bacon and hash-browns are about ready too. The players will be lining up soon for breakfast. You can dish out the porridge; we will bring the coffee and the rest of the hot food out and set it up here." She pointed towards the empty trestle table behind me.

"Dish out the porridge?" I repeated. "As in serve the players?"

"You don't want them eating out of the pot, do you?" Margaret said, laughing. "I think you need more coffee, Gillian."

"Ha, ha." I laughed weakly. Of course I would be serving food. Why hadn't I thought of that? What if Ralph spotted me? Or even Lauren? My plan had been just to check things out, observe from a distance.

Now how would I explain to Ralph my sudden appearance standing over a hot cauldron, dishing out porridge to the masses? Or to Lauren? *Hey, do you mind not mentioning to Ralph that you saw me?* For not the last time, I anticipated a few flaws with my spy plan.

More kitchen volunteers streamed outside, carrying the other breakfast items and setting up another cauldron – this time filled with coffee – on a tripod over a second fire. I rolled my eyes. That coffee had just come out of a twenty-first-century urn. Who were we kidding? Besides, please explain to me how these medieval knights got the coffee beans out here without modern day freight trains or airplanes or ships or whatever was used to import that stuff.

Okay, Gill. I gave myself a shake. The anxiety over what to say to Ralph was creeping back. What a stupid idea this was anyway. Why did I listen to Torres? Or maybe I should've listened better...it wouldn't be weird if Ralph knew I was down here in "support" of his hobby.

As Margaret had predicted, the PCs started making their way down for breakfast. Another volunteer came to help me out. She handed me a bowl and I filled it and in turn handed it to one of the players. Other than constantly scanning the line for my husband, it wasn't too difficult. After the initial group of characters were served, there was a lull in the lineup. I used the break to pull my hood over top of my head.

"A little cold out here," I said in explanation.

The other volunteer smiled. She looked to be in her early twenties, and I wondered what would attract someone her age to volunteer for larp. Surely there were interesting dance clubs in the city?

"So," I asked, "do you have a boyfriend down here? Or perhaps you're looking?"

"I'm looking," she said with a grin. Her name was Micah, and this was her third time at a larp event.

"I like your dress. It's very lovely."

"Thanks! I bought it online. Deer hide. Hand embroidered. It's great until about noon. Then I change into something a bit lighter." Micah's azure dress was indeed exquisite and was definitely a notch above my rented homespun. She had piled her long auburn hair in a droopy bun high on her head. Her eyes were rimmed in black eyeliner, and I wondered what time she was up to look so well put together this early in the morning. I patted my own frizzy brown hair.

Another group of players rounded the corner and I did a quick scan of their faces. No Ralph. As we served the new group, I considered my options. Could I somehow skip out? Could I run to the bathroom and leave Micah with the porridge duties? Or maybe it was just better to say, "Morning, Ralph. Would you like some porridge?"

Yes. That was what I should do. Get it over with. Make it clear it was no big deal I was out here. I just wanted to be supportive of his hobby; learn a little more about it. I felt a sense of calmness about this option and knew it was the right thing to do. Probably, we'd have some coffee together and laugh about how surprised he was to see me.

I ladled out another serving of hot porridge and handed the bowl to the next person in line. But instead of taking the bowl and muttering thanks like everyone else, a warm hand firmly embraced mine, keeping it trapped against the bowl.

"Uh, excuse me." I stammered. I gave a slight tug of my hand, but no use.

"Good morning, Gretchen, my sweet." Startled, I looked up. I had been so focused on what to say to Ralph that I hadn't thought about other people I might know.

"Oh. Um, hi there." I tried to pull my hand back, but he

still wouldn't let go. "Good to see you again, Ivan. The Great."

He smiled and squeezed my hand tighter against the bowl. The lineup had come to a standstill; Micah and everyone else nearby was watching in rapt attention as my face flamed. Good God.

"The Wanderer," he corrected.

"Pardon?"

"Ivan the Wanderer. My eye. It wanders."

I let out a hideous shriek of laughter, straight from my grade eight depths. "Wow. You certainly took me unawares. Well, all the very best in your wanders, my friend. Here. Your porridge." Yes, I was blathering now. I pushed our clasped hands and porridge towards him.

Ivan gave my hand one last squeeze. "Yes, my sweet Gretchen. I shall see you at noon."

"Adieu…scoundrel." I waved goodbye. I knew I shouldn't encourage him, but there was something very surreal and funny about the whole thing.

I continued in my serving duties as best I could. The man behind Ivan grinned at me, but no one else tried to accost me. An odd, giddy feeling ebbed through my veins. Strange.

As soon as we hit another break in the lineup, Micah dug her elbow into my ribs. I looked over at her.

"Wow!" She grinned. "Ivan! How did you land that one?"

Land him? I don't know…how had I? Married women didn't usually go about landing strange men in forests.

"Oh, I'm definitely not looking to land anyone." I held up my hand and showed her my plain, utilitarian wedding band. "I think he – you know, men like him – enjoy having a damsel in distress to rescue. Or something. I'm not sure. I had a weird encounter yesterday and he helped me, that's all."

She gave me a sceptical look. I was surprised she wasn't having any luck. Measuring myself against Micah, I came out on the middle-aged, less curvy end of the stick, and I'd practically been accosted upon entering the camp.

Perhaps Jas should try this larp thing. Then again, I could not see her hooking up with anyone sporting weekend armour. Oh right, that was me who was married to the weekend armour.

Micah and I continued to serve the porridge, and nothing else remarkable happened. She seemed to know a few of the players, and I let her handle the small talk while I watched the crowd. She had her mission, and I had mine. No need getting in her way.

Before I knew it, Ralph was sauntering around the last bend of trees on the path leading to the kitchen. He wore similar garb to the knights: forest-green leggings and shirt underneath shoulder armour and a chest plate with a rearing stallion emblazoned across it.

Despite the absurdity of wearing armour in the twenty-first century, he did look rather dashing. I felt a small tenderness for him. I was used to seeing him in casual business clothes or shorts and T-shirt mowing the lawn. This side of him was completely different and boyish in comparison. Maybe this whole larp thing really was just a harmless hobby. Maybe I had been making way too big a deal of it.

Grinning, I prepared to surprise him. It was going to be okay.

But that's when I noticed who he was walking next to.

His companion wore long leather chaps that accentuated lean and toned thighs. Her tightly fitted chest plate and arm coverings were made from black leather. A cape hung from her shoulders in crimson red, a sharp contrast to her shimmering blonde hair. Lauren.

Although Ralph was walking in my direction, he still hadn't seen me. That was because his face was turned towards Lauren, listening to whatever she was saying. It felt like a chunk of ice had hit the pit of my stomach. I felt fat and ugly in my bulky layers and slept-on hair.

"Micah," I said, handing her the serving spoon, "can you do this for a few minutes? I, I need to go in. I feel, um, dizzy. Need to sit for a minute."

"Are you okay?" Concern spread across her face, but I had no time to explain. And what would I say, anyway?

"I'm, uh, fine. I think I need to sit a minute. See if it passes." She took the ladle and I hightailed it back into the kitchen, down the corridor, and into the deserted volunteer bathroom. No cellphone to call Jas. No window to peep out from to see what was happening. Just me and my humiliation.

Did this mean anything? And if it did, why was I upset? Hadn't I been thinking life might be better on my own? Wasn't this marriage lacking anything that brought life and meaning? Had I not been contemplating what it would be like to find love and excitement all over again, the way that Jas was getting to do?

Jas was right. I hadn't been happy in a long time. Watching her interaction with Daniel had awakened something in me. I wanted someone who was interested in me. Excited about me. And that no longer seemed a possibility in my marriage, regardless of Torres's ridiculous ideas. You couldn't just create that kind of feeling with a little goodwill.

Not when there was so much gurgling and rolling and maddening water under the bridge. And Ralph and I were practically drowning in water.

So now, when it seemed like I might have an out, why on earth would I be a sobbing mess in some freezing toilet stall in a godforsaken campground? *Really, Gill. Wasn't this what you wanted?* A way out, and I didn't even have to look like the bad guy.

Chapter Eighteen

I returned to the kitchen in time to help with clean up. I'm sure my eyes were red rimmed, but no one commented. The PCs had, for the most part, finished their breakfast and returned to cavorting in the woods. In fact, only a few magical creatures were still lounging around, chewing on the last pieces of bacon. And most of them were green. I knew enough to avoid that crowd.

After downing my own quick breakfast of fruit, bacon, dry toast and absolutely none of the porridge-turned-gluey-mess, I picked up a tea towel and joined the women who were drying dishes. Before long, I felt a hand squeeze my shoulder from behind.

"Are you feeling okay?" Margaret asked.

"Oh, yes. I think it passed. I sometimes get migraines when the weather changes. And my allergies are acting up...you know, hay fever." I rapidly blinked my eyes as though they were itchy. If at some point I did decide to tuck my medieval kitchen wench tail between my legs and hightail it back to civilization, I'd already have a preconceived excuse. For now, I was pissed off enough to want to get to the bottom of whatever I'd seen. Was my husband using larp to hide some kind of relationship from me?

I gave my head a shake and tried to focus on Margaret, who was still talking to me. "Just let me know if you need to lie down." Concern was etched on her face and I nodded. "We do not want you to have a miserable time out here. And I could make you some soothing willow bark tea if you think that would help with the migraine? It's remarkably effective."

"Oh! Willow bark…how kind. I've actually tried a," I lowered my voice before continuing, "modern remedy in the washroom." Besides, this was my exit strategy she was messing with.

After completing the morning dishes, a woman who seemed to be one of the organisers called all the volunteers together. After thanking everyone for putting on a hearty breakfast, she handed out bright orange wristbands.

"If anyone is interested in checking out the game that's in play, you need to wear one of these," she said. "It will keep you visible to the players, and they will know that you can't be used to influence the outcome of the game in any way. Another option is to join Jody – Jody, wave your hand, please; she's right over here, ladies – who's offered to teach everyone how to knot your own fishing net out of jute! Isn't that lovely? It's a great opportunity to learn a dying trade as well as view the game in an unobtrusive way.

"Again, thanks to everyone for volunteering your time this weekend, especially our first-timers." She paused to wink in my direction. "Remember: lunch is self-serve; sandwich station is already set up. You don't need to be back in the kitchen until you hear three consecutive bangs on this cymbal." She held up a large brass cymbal and hit it with a furry mallet. I wondered how far the sound would carry. "When you hear that, it means it's time to come back and start preparing the dinner menu."

Right. Three bangs. I wanted to shout, *Do you know how much easier this would be if you just used a damn clock?* But it wasn't their fault my marriage sucked. Anyway, I now had a ready-made window for stalking my husband. Fantastic.

As the group dispersed, Micah, the young woman I'd left on porridge duty, approached. "Are you feeling okay?" she asked.

"Oh. All right, I guess. It seems to have passed. For now." She nodded as though what I'd said made any kind of sense. "Sorry about leaving you like that."

"No problem. Did you want to walk around the camp? If

you're feeling up to it, that is. Or were you planning on making a fishing net?"

"Tempting, but no. I'm strongly leaning towards walking around the camp. What about you?"

"I'm not likely to meet a guy while tying knots." Micah smiled and gestured towards the door.

"That's likely true," I said, following her outside. "Let's get you laid. I mean, let's find you a strong handsome man to pay the bills."

Micah giggled, and we set out in a group with four or five other women. They were a variety of ages, and I assumed some would be on the lookout for their family members. And so was I.

We'd tied the orange bands on our wrists, but they weren't that visible as most of us were wearing shawl-inspired cloaks in order to keep warm in the cooler morning air. But, worst case, we could flash them easily enough, assuming we weren't hit by a rubber-tipped arrow from behind.

The sun was currently hidden behind the clouds, and a low-lying fog had settled in about the tree trunks and damp grasses. I fastened my cape and pulled my hood over my head in an attempt to block the cold out.

My group turned down the path in the opposite direction I had travelled last night, heading deeper into the campsite. I was happy to follow the more experienced women; they seemed to know where they were headed, and I had no idea where Ralph might be. As the group chatted away, I was also content to stay silent, spending my time peering out from under my hood at anyone passing by.

We stopped to witness a skirmish. One of the women in our group cheered for a man she seemed to know. I looked around. All the other volunteers were watching the fight with rapt attention. Didn't anyone else think this was odd? It didn't appear that way. I felt an outsider; I could not reconcile this pastime with normal hobbies.

Although other than my possibly two-timing husband, there didn't seem to be anything immoral about it. And people generally seemed to be enjoying themselves. Certainly more than if they were racing around the city getting errands done.

We walked on, our ears picking up the sound of music before we could see where it originated from. Turning onto a flat grassy meadow, we discovered a small group of musicians played a lyrical – if a bit rusty – ballad. One played a mandolin-type instrument, another a wooden lute or recorder, and a third padded out the tempo on a hand drum. The instruments were likely as authentic as my rental tunic, but it made me smile.

"Are those musicians paid to be here?" I whispered to Micah.

"I doubt it. They're likely either NPCs like us or players who get some health points for contributing to the general atmosphere."

I was about to ask another question when an arm wrapped around Micah's waist and drew her into the semicircle formed by the audience of PCs and NPCs. As the man pulled Micah into some kind of wretched jig dance, the musicians picked up their tempo. Micah appeared to waffle between embarrassment and pleasure, and before long, the rest of us were clapping our hands and laughing (in my case, laughing with sweet relief that it hadn't been me).

But above the sound of the happy ballad, angry voices drew my attention. I looked around. The meadow we were standing in was rimmed with trees and dense undergrowth, but at the far end of the open field, a group of armoured characters appeared to be in the midst of a standoff. I hadn't noticed the players earlier; whether they had just entered the field or their negotiations had just become more heated, I couldn't say.

The group was divided between forest-green and scarlet costumes, and the disagreement was quickly turning into a pushing match. I looked back at my volunteer companions, but no one else seemed to be interested. They all still cheered Micah on as her dance partner attempted to manoeuvre her into what looked a seriously unstable dip.

I looked back towards the escalating conflict just in time to see it. My heart stopped. Because there, running away from the group, was Ralph in forest-green cloak and chest armour, with long blonde hair and a red cape running beside him. They seemed to be escaping the escalating conflict by entering the woods that surrounded the meadow.

Micah danced. The other volunteers cheered and clapped their hands in time with the drummer. As for me, I quietly stepped away from the group and edged towards tree cover. This was my chance. Faster than I'd expected, but here it was. I had to take it.

Scurrying away from the clearing, I tried not to trip on my floor-length homespun. I entered the shadowed tree cover and thankfully spotted a narrow footpath in the general direction I'd seen Ralph and the blonde bitch head. I picked up my skirts and ran.

It was several hundred metres and two near-spills on tree roots before my brain caught up. *What are you doing?* it screamed at me. *Have you noticed you are running down a deer track in homespun and leather, chasing after your husband and his possible lover, who is ten years younger and potentially forty pounds slimmer? And what, pray tell, will you do if you actually catch them?*

I had no answers. I just knew that I had to run; I had to find out. This might be my only chance to discover the truth.

Chapter Nineteen

My heart was pounding out a furious tempo as my burning thighs hammered through the forest. Dodging tree trunks, knobbly roots and thorny bushes, I kept my eyes trained for any sign of Ralph or of Lauren's crimson cape receding in the distance. If it weren't for the seething jealousy fuelling me, I'd have already succumbed to the lactic acid building up in my legs.

My constricted lungs and raspy breath could be attributed to my current lack of cardiovascular health, but truth be told, the agony of rejection was equally to blame. I didn't need a session with Torres to know I was on the verge of hysteria. Yes, I was being dramatic. Weak and alone and dramatic.

Slowing down, I took a quick look at my surroundings. I'd lost sight of them and I stopped to listen for any clues. I could hear the outbreak of skirmishes in the distance. The grassy meadow where the musicians had played was out of sight, but their music still floated in the air. I could hear nothing closer at hand except the random chatter of squirrels.

A wide swathe of heavy shrub surrounded the meadow and I'd made my way through it at a diagonal, thanks to the help of the footpath. Ahead of me, the trees were thinning out considerably and that was the direction I figured I needed to head if I wanted to continue with my pursuit of Ralph and his...friend.

There. Ahead in the distance. I spotted the bright red of Lauren's cape peeking out from the foliage. They were travelling towards an area of the campground where I hadn't yet been.

I pulled the hood of my cloak over my head and held it tightly under my chin as I continued to jog, this time at a slower pace. The trees thinned almost entirely and the land sloped down into a ravine. I found refuge behind a large boulder and, peeking above it, could see an encampment.

Six crimson-and-black marquee-style tents were set up in the valley. Could the colours represent a specific team or army? Yes, I thought so. On one tent hung a banner with the stencilled outline of an eight-legged spider. It was identical to the one I'd spotted on Lauren's chest plate last night.

Several players were mingling, cleaning off weapons, deliberating over maps. Good God. This was really insane.

Still walking side by side, Ralph and Lauren entered the camp. Ralph turned and laughed at something she'd said. I couldn't hear what it was, but I could see his profile. Ralph looked relaxed and happy and very much at ease. Definitely not how he looked at home. My heart squeezed. The sound of his laughter was misery; it seemed like years since he'd laughed as easily with me.

And then, to my utter disbelief – although how on earth could I possibly disbelieve anything anymore? – Ralph turned towards one of the tents and held open the entrance flap for Lauren. She entered and he followed.

A terrible stab of pain shot through my core. What was going on? In my marriage. With my husband. In that tent.

Knowing it could very well be anything, from some secret dumb-ass larp strategising all the way to something entirely more intimate, I was overcome with a need to find out. My body started walking, then running, in the direction of the tent. Granted, my frozen heart was still back behind the boulder in child's pose, likely hanging out with my now-comatose brain (which, honestly, could have put a wee bit more effort into reasoning me out of this). As for my body, it was nearly at the lip of the ravine, ready to hurl itself down towards the tent.

I was so intent on my goal, I didn't hear the running footsteps. Didn't hear the whoosh of the boffer or the triumphant yell as the large Styrofoam sledgehammer took me full force in the chest. But I did feel the intense surprise when I was suddenly thrown full force on my back, the air completely knocked out of my lungs.

Heaving on the ground, struggling to catch my breath, I was dimly aware of being dragged back behind the boulder.

Chapter Twenty

Lying flat on my back, I looked up. Looked straight into the eyes of the elderly costume shop owner. I watched as recognition slowly dawned on her face, replacing all traces of glee from her takedown. Her eyes travelled down my costume, confirming that it was in fact rented from her, before settling back on my face.

Which shouldn't have been hard to recognise in the first place, seeing as it'd been less than a week since I was in her store. Furthermore, I essentially looked to be the same person: I was not wearing any costume makeup or face-altering appliances – the same of which could *not* be said for her.

Not only was she sporting the pointy elf-shaped ears she sold at the shop, her face was painted a bright green. Great. My archenemy, come to get me again.

As the air slowly returned to my lungs, I took in a little more of my surroundings. We were back within the tree line, behind the boulder, and bent down in the shrubbery – we were hidden from the camp in the ravine. Which wasn't a bad thing; I wasn't sure that Ralph and Lauren discovering me lying in the dirt was quite what I had in mind when I first began my sprint of rage. Not that a firm plan had really been established, but still.

I weakly held up my wrist to show my neon-orange NPC band. "I'm a kitchen volunteer, remember?"

"I'm sorry. I couldn't see your wristband at all, what with your cloak on." She seemed distressed and bewildered. And indignant. "What on earth are you doing so far out in the gaming area?"

"Me? What, for god-freakin'-sake, are you doing hiding

in the woods accosting innocent volunteers?" I absently wondered if there was a penalty for hitting a volunteer.

She looked left and right before answering in hushed tones. "I'm on a recon mission. Observe and report back. It doesn't usually involve marks, but you were charging through the forest as though nothing was at stake. And a straight shot like that? Seventeen body points – if you hadn't been a volunteer, obviously."

I wasn't quite ready to get up yet, and I wasn't sure how to respond to a statement like that anyway, so I silently continued to lie unmoving in the dirt. Which was fine, because she had more to say.

"When I saw you charging in with your brown cloak flapping about…well, I thought you were here to broker a deal with the other human camp, and we elves couldn't have that. And by the way, why *were* you hell-bent on entering headquarters?"

Headquarters? That must be the name of this group of tents. "A little recon of my own, you could say." She immediately looked suspicious. "Of a personal nature. Seriously. No gameplay involved." I used my elbows to prop myself up and, seeing that the dizziness had passed, slowly got on my feet.

"Dry cleaning is an extra five dollars on the bill, you know." I looked up and held her gaze as I dusted grass and weeds off my backside. I was completely incredulous.

My elven attacker–*slash*–costume supplier was hedging silently back towards the forest cover, and I realised she didn't want to be seen by the people in the headquarters camp. Did I? The reality of the situation – the real one involving my marriage and my husband – hit me anew, and it no longer seemed wise to race in to face betrayal, demanding…what? Answers? I decided to do the only thing that made sense at this point. I decided to follow the elf.

"Hey," I said in hushed tones when I caught up with her. "Could you, um, direct me back towards the kitchen area? I really have no sense of where it is anymore." She turned but looked nervous. Perhaps that would risk her character? "Or to the glade where the musicians are playing? I can find my way from there."

"Sure. That will work. It's a neutral zone. So is the area where we eat our meals. But you've got to stay quiet. Stealthy. Do as I say, got it?"

"Whatever you say." I had no energy to do more than agree. I hadn't yet heard the three bangs on the kitchen cymbal announcing it was time to begin dinner preparations, didn't even know if I'd hear it this far out. I was completely emotionally drained.

We made our way back along several footpaths through the wooded area. It took a lot longer than when I was racing hell-bent in the opposite direction as my guide would pause ever so often and listen for sounds that might indicate enemy pursuit.

"So, um, I didn't catch your name."

"My game name is Glenna, but," she froze and raised her hand for silence. I listened to the forest around us, searching the trees for movement. But when nothing untoward happened, we continued on our way. "You probably mean my real name. It's Rosie. Normally I would be staying in character the whole weekend, you understand? But it's just this encounter that's thrown me off. If you see me again out here, I'll act like I don't know you and like I don't even speak English. It's really intense."

"I can imagine." After several minutes walking in silence, we arrived at the edge of the glade where the musicians were packing up their instruments.

I turned and thanked her for leading me back, and she apologised for game-killing me on my first weekend as a volunteer. I somewhat graciously accepted. Who knows? Maybe she had only delayed the inevitable, but at least I could now plan an actual strategy.

"What keeps you larping?" I asked Rosie in farewell. "You don't find it exhausting?"

She grinned under her green paint, her teeth astoundingly white in comparison. "Bleep peep!" she said and walked back into the woods.

Chapter Twenty-One

Despite my desperate adventure, I still managed to make it back to the OOP area before any of the other women I'd set out walking with. Another group of volunteers, including Margaret, were sitting by a picnic table drinking coffee and knotting fishing nets on makeshift looms. Margaret waved and I waved back but quickly escaped into the now-deserted sleeping quarters.

I was relieved that no one was around. On my bunk was my zipped-up duffle bag. I immediately opened it and started rifling through, desperate for the contraband I'd hidden there. On the bottom, underneath my spare underwear, sunscreen, and hairbrush, I dug out my forbidden twenty-first-century cellphone. It seemed a lifeline to sanity. I turned it on, and as it was powering up I kissed the screen. I was so thankful to live in a time when contact with a rational friend was an easy text away.

I lay down on my bunk with my back to the room, not wanting to get caught by any other volunteers entering the dorm (Although what would they do? Take my phone away? I doubted it.) Holding the phone close to my face, I waited for it to power up so that I could contact Jas and pour out my heart.

No! No cellular signal! Not even one tiny bar! Damn this valley campground. I could die out here, slit my wrists or hang myself from the kitchen rafters, and there was no way to notify the authorities. Worse yet, I could discover my husband was having an affair and not be able to contact the one person I could count on to see me through this.

Damn it. My last hope evaporated. I would have to figure this out on my own. I stuffed the phone into my bodice so I could try later when I was outside. Surely there was somewhere else I could find reception?

I lay there all alone in a borrowed camp bunk that had seen decades of children at summer camp, women on retreats, and churchgoers at bible camp and let the tears fall. They streamed over my nose and puddled on my sleeping bag, silently soaking my hair at my temples.

In the distance I could hear people preparing their lunch at the self-serve station that had been set up earlier. I wasn't hungry. Food, and forced conversation with strangers, were the last things I wanted right now.

Through my misery, my conscious squeaked out taunts:

If you really came out here to build connection in your marriage, then why didn't you tell him you were coming?

Because, I said to my damn conscious, I'm here to find the truth, remember?

So you don't trust him. Why else would you be spying?

Maybe I'm looking for a way out. To collect evidence that would prove the problem in our marriage isn't me.

Then why do you care what he's doing? If that's what you really want, shouldn't you be happy, Gill?

But I wasn't happy. I was aching and miserable. How could he? After all these years, how could he do this to me? Slowly I fell into a restless nap, and tried not to think. The time slipped by until I heard an obnoxious banging. It was the damn dinner cymbal.

Great. I rubbed my eyes with my fists and sat up. I'd stay at the camp. For now. But I had to formulate a plan. Decide if it was wiser to confront him here, where the evidence was, or wait until I was on home turf. Or, said that small nagging voice, you could do nothing. *You could pretend you never saw anything. And what did you see, anyway?*

I could hear volunteers streaming back into the kitchen and roles for dinner prep already being assigned. Before joining the other volunteers, I slipped into the bathroom to check how my face looked. Could you tell I'd been crying? My eyes were red rimmed, but other than that, the misery inside didn't seem to be manifested externally.

Once in the kitchen, I was assigned to potato peeling with Margaret and two other women. We had a giant heap to get through, and potato by potato I listened to them chatter while silently nursing my inner turmoil.

The woman peeling beside me asked, "Have you heard anything about how the mission is going?"

I couldn't tell if she was searching for small talk or was actually interested. Regardless, I'd only one possible response.

I shrugged. "Not sure."

"I overheard something about a spy being detained for questioning back at headquarters," said Margaret. "I bet they'll need to barter him back or conduct a raid in order to rescue him from the enemy forces."

At the word *headquarters*, my ears perked up. That was the name Rosie had used to refer to the small grouping of tents, wasn't it?

"Who are the enemy forces?" I asked. The three women looked over at my sudden interest in game play.

"They're the players in black and crimson," said Margaret. "They usually have some type of spider on their armour or shields. They're basically a hoard of half humans who are hell-bent on stealing the royal sceptre from the Horsemen's Army. It'll increase their power," she said, giving me what I sensed was the Coles Notes version. "The Horsemen are the ones in green."

"Oh. Right." I could hear it in my own voice. The flat effect that made it sound as though I didn't care. And of course, I didn't. Although I now knew which pretend armies Ralph and Lauren belonged too, I didn't see how that could help me. If I understood correctly, they were enemies and therefore had even less reason to be prancing about the country together.

The mountain of peeled and cut potatoes grew steadily until the last skinny brown skin had been removed. I listened to the women chatter on about the direction of the game and about a twisted ankle on one of the magicians, but

I did not join the discussion.

Soon enough, the potatoes were put in water to boil and I was assigned to another group. This one involved basting and rotating chickens as they roasted over the outdoor fire-pits. It was like Swiss Chalet, but a thousand years ago.

Back outside the day had warmed, and I took off my over-cloak. It was funny, I realised, I no longer cared who recognised me, no longer worried about Ralph sauntering by and spotting me. Not that he was sauntering around anyway. Nope. He was back in headquarters. In some tent. Screwing my co-worker! I swallowed back a sob. *Get a grip, Campbell!* I basted the three damned chicken carcasses hanging off the spit in front of me.

"Are you okay?" a voice behind me asked. It was Micah. "We couldn't find you this afternoon."

I stifled my anger and used my sleeve to wipe the tear forming at the corner of my eye.

"Actually, no, I'm not fine." The other volunteers had headed back inside to cut chicken; there was only my last spit still sizzling away. But I couldn't seem to keep it together. "I'm…I'm really sorry. I, I just find myself at a bit of a crossroads." Micah put her hand on my shoulder, which was a bit strange considering I'd only met her this morning, but I was upset, and it was really kind. Kind enough that I started sobbing in earnest.

"It's cancer, isn't it," said Micah.

"Pardon?" I rubbed my nose on my sleeve.

"The crossroads. It's cancer. I just knew it." Micah leaned over and gave me a big hug. I didn't know what to do, but my tears turned into demented giggling, which was really inappropriate given she thought I was dying from a terrible disease.

"I'm sorry, Micah. But, um, I'm, ah, cancer-free. To the best of my knowledge." I gave her a pat on the back and she released me, although she didn't look as though she entirely believed me. "That was really kind of you, though. I really appreciate your caring. It's, um, something else."

I dried my eyes roughly on my homespun sleeve. I could

feel the tears were not far from the surface, but at least they weren't still pouring down my face. "My...my husband." I took several inhales of fresh air, trying to cleanse my lungs and get a grip. "He is here. At larp. He...he doesn't know that I am here, you know, working in the kitchen. I've never come on a larp before, never let on that I was interested. Not that I am! I'm kind of using the volunteer opportunity to check it out without committing.

"But then I saw him today." My voice was rambling, getting choppy. I stopped to take a deep breath to control my emotions, but the words kept flowing. "I saw him going into a tent with another woman."

Micah's eyes didn't get wide or show any sign of surprise as I'd expected. But then, she was in her early twenties. Younger people had more interesting lives, filled with intense sex and multiple partners, if half of what I saw on television was true.

"The thing is, Micah, we've been married for, like, fifteen years. We don't have kids. It's just him and I. And things have been, well, strained for some time. But I guess I didn't anticipate he would get involved with someone else."

"But now you think he is?"

"Like I said, I saw him going into a tent with another woman! And get this – she works with me! He's never told me he actually hangs out *with* her at these larp things!"

Micah nodded. "And...something happened on the way into the tent that spelled it all out for you? He pulled her close to him, looked into her eyes. And you knew!"

"Well. Not exactly. He, ah, held the tent flap open."

"And kissed her!"

"God, no!"

"As she knelt down to get into the tent, he smacked her on the ass?"

Who the hell was I confiding in? "Micah, I'm middle-aged. I've lived practically my whole adult life with this guy. I just saw him hold the tent flap open for her, and she walked in and he followed. It happened at headquarters. And this morning, over breakfast? It wasn't my allergies at

127

all! I'm sorry to have left you like that, but I had to get away. They were talking. Walking down that path together!" I held out my arm and pointed at the offending pathway.

"And they were holding hands. And he leaned over and —"

"No!"

Micah squinted her eyes. Surely a sign of deeper contemplation. "I'm sorry, I'm a bit confused. I'm sure you know your own husband, Gillian. But, um, people here have to stay in character at all times. How do you know they weren't roleplaying a mission or something? Like that guy this morning – Ivan the Ingrate."

"The Wanderer," I corrected.

"Sure. The Wanderer. You don't think he acts like that every day, do you? He's probably some uptight lawyer with a pickle up his ass. Or maybe he's even gay! Or a total introvert who would never, in a billion weeks, approach a woman. Larp is about taking on another character and completely living their life over the weekend." Micah stopped for a moment, letting me catch up to her train of thought. "What I'm saying is, you didn't actually see your husband. You saw your husband pretending to be someone else."

My heart dropped. "Completely living their life? Do you think…do you think they've got this massive sexual relationship going on, and they justify it because they aren't actually Ralph and Lauren but are some horny warrior types?!" I was hyperventilating.

Micah broke out into gales of laughter. "This isn't an orgy! It's larp! There are ground rules here, Gillian!"

I'd confided my fears to Micah but was now even more confused. Had I actually seen what I thought I'd seen, or had my interpretation been wrong?

But there was no time left to talk about it. Margaret was calling from the kitchen. "Are you ladies coming in with those chickens already? We've got an army to feed in twenty minutes!"

"Coming," I called back before turning to Micah. "How

do I look?"

Micah studied my face. "Like you've been standing over a fire. If anyone says your eyes are red, just say the smoke bothers them. Or stick to that hay fever bit you used earlier."

We each picked up an end of the spit, the three roasted chickens sizzling in the middle, and started carrying it back towards the kitchen. Hot juices dripped onto the dirt, leaving a trail of chicken grease in our wake.

"Um, thanks, Micah. I feel, you know, better having confided in someone. I have a lot to consider. Just need to figure out what I'm going to do next."

"More research, of course. We're going to find him, figure out what's going on, and if it's really what you think, well, we'll totally cyborg his ass!"

Good Lord, I didn't even know what that meant, but I felt like cheering inside. This kid was nearly half my age and had likely never sustained a relationship for twelve consecutive months, and I was fully prepared to take advice from her. I had found my very own Little John, and we were going to crack this wide open. The truth would be revealed.

At that thought, despair squeezed my throat, but I breathed through it. There was only one way forward now. And a tiny flame of hope still flickered. Obviously, Micah thought I could be misinterpreting what was going on. And maybe I was. A second pair of eyes would definitely help in getting to the bottom of this.

Depositing our loaded spit at the carving station, I looked around. The kitchen crew moved like a well-oiled trebuchet, and I rolled up my sleeves, prepared to help anywhere I could. I wanted to get through this meal and onto Micah's plan.

As the players trickled into the outdoor eating area, we prepared to serve the meal. I was on potato duty, and I scooped as fast as I could, which wasn't too fast because the chicken lady in front of me seemed to be having a conversation with everyone. Micah, who was with me on potatoes, leaned over to whisper in my ear.

129

"If you see him – or her – you've got to take off before they see you. If they know you're here, I won't be able to guarantee the validity of our results."

I gave her a funny look. "That sounds very sciencey."

"I'm a chem major."

"Oh." Case in point, I guess. People with very regular lives came out to these things. And I doubted many of her profs or university peers knew she was dressed in a deer-hide dress this particular weekend.

We got through the dinner rush with no sign of Ralph. I didn't know what that meant, but my heart feared the worst. Could he be too busy rolling around naked in a tent with his lover to come for food? But, no, that couldn't be because there was Lauren, strolling towards the food line with a confident swagger. "There she is," I whispered to Micah. "Red cape." I took cover in the kitchen and peeked out the window.

Sure enough. No Ralph. What did that mean? I searched the crowd. There was Rosie with her group of green friends, keeping to themselves. They were twittering and eating, and I couldn't help but smile as I rubbed my bruised chest. She must be the oldest person out here, and she looked absurd and happy at the same time.

Unsure if it was safe to go back outside, I got started washing the dirty trenchers that were already being dropped off. Margaret came to help, and before long, another volunteer came to take my place so that I could take a turn eating my own meal.

Having skipped lunch, my stomach was growling for nourishment. Besides, I'd need energy for whatever Micah had planned for tonight. I bolted down one last piece of chicken, wiped the grease off my fingers, then grabbed my hooded cloak before meeting Micah back outside.

Seeing as our duties were complete, we informed Margaret we were going out to explore and observe the game in process. Although it was open territory for NPCs, it seemed a good idea to let someone know where we were. We did not, after all, have a flashlight or phone with us, and who knows what dangers – either real or imagined – might be waiting for us.

"Where was the last place you saw him again?" Micah asked as we headed back down the path towards the meadow.

"Headquarters."

"And you think you could find headquarters?" I nodded. "Okay. Let's head in that direction, and let me do the talking, okay? Remember, we need to stay in character at all times. It's not really fair to the game or the other players if we don't."

"Okay. What's our story?"

"We are kitchen wenches. Out for an evening stroll. Perhaps even damsels in distress who need help finding our way. Do you know what your husband's character name is?"

"God, no."

"How long has he been doing live action?"

"A year or so."

"And you don't know his game name?"

I winced. Perhaps I should have shown a little interest.

"I haven't really shared his passion for this particular pastime. It's been…a tough year."

Micah nodded and didn't ask more. Learning from my experience this afternoon, we walked at a leisurely pace, as though on an evening stroll. It was hard to do; I wanted to race back to our destination in case we were missing anything important. But instead we ambled on, making sure our wristbands stayed in clear view of those who passed by us.

The road was busy. Groups of fighters ran by in the opposite direction, carrying clubs, dulled spears, and PVC pipes wrapped in blankets and affixed in place with duct tape. Many wore similar colours to Ralph and displayed the rearing horse insignia on their shields or chest plates. Others sported crimson, and still others wore a random mix of medieval and fantastical creature garb.

I spotted the woman with butterflies attached to her eyebrows, the one I had first seen when entering the camp yesterday. A quiver of rubber-tipped arrows and a bow were still slung across her back. Were they for show or did she use them? I wondered if it was out of the question for NPCs to carry weapons – and use them on their husbands.

With a smile plastered on her face, Micah looped her arm through mine as though we were on a schoolgirl jaunt. "Look like you are having fun," she said through gritted teeth, her lips pinned back in an overly effusive smile.

"Why?" I said, but I made a similar expression of my own.

"We are supposed to stay in character when we are in the games area, right? It helps the game feel more real to everyone if we participate as our characters, too. And we are kitchen workers, young attractive kitchen workers out for a walk after a long day working the fires."

I wanted to ask if it really mattered, but I knew Micah was into this whole roleplaying thing more than I was. And so I tried to look happy. And young. And attractive. Perhaps I wasn't very convincing because Micah continued, "If we don't stay in character and players complain about us, we might not be able to return." This argument weighed heavier on me because I didn't want to repay Micah's kindness by getting her kicked out of the local larp club.

"We're pretty safe as long as we stay along this road." By road, Micah referred to the paved pathway that ran through the campsite. "But as soon as we wander into the forest, we could be mistaken for spies or players, as you were this afternoon. We can always show our wristbands, but it's easier if we just try to stay out of people's way. We have a mission tonight!"

For Micah, this was excitement. It didn't mean the possible end of her life outside the camp and involved no major turning point. I was overcome by what might happen and just let her lead me.

A few times men catcalled or we were challenged by various factions. Micah called out in a fake cockney accent, and we flashed our NPC neon-orange bracelets when needed. It seemed the atmosphere was a lot tenser than it had been this morning, but I didn't give it much thought.

As we approached the meadow where the musicians had been performing this morning, we again heard the sound of folk music. This time an accordion player was providing the entertainment. I looked sceptically at her instrument – I was no expert when it came to accordions, but it looked decidedly modern to me. If those were the rules we were playing by, I should, by rights, be allowed to access a corded rotary phone out here.

Standing with the small audience, I focused on getting my orientation correct; I was pretty certain I'd entered the forest right behind where I was currently standing. I leaned over and whispered in Micah's ear, "This way to headquarters." When she looked, I pointed towards the entrance to the footpath that snaked through the forested region.

As one, we turned towards the path. But before we took more than two steps, a large armoured body suddenly stood in front of me, thrusting a small bouquet of wildflowers into my face.

"For you, my sweet Gretchen, the most beautiful of wenchens." Ivan's voice boomed, and I couldn't believe my bad luck for coming up with the most ludicrous of names ever. My face was a flaming tomato.

"Thank you, Ivan. Er…isn't it illegal to pick wildflowers?" I said. But a sidelong look at Micah's bulging eyes reminded me of the whole stay in character rule, and so I attempted a quick back pedal.

"What I mean to say, oh Great Wanderer, is that, didn't the…king decree a law against wildflower picking?"

"Have your wits been addled, milady? The king is dead! And even if he weren't, I don't think his vile heart was concerned with flowers. Do you?"

"Ah, no, no. Of course." Reaching out, I accepted his offer, which seemed to somewhat alleviate the concern on his brow. "These are lovely. And yes, I did sustain an injury only this afternoon. I am, most certainly, a bit addled." What the hell? But Micah and Ivan were both smiling, so I must've said the right thing.

Ivan swooped in, placing one hand on my hip and folding the other around the wrist of my hand that clutched the flowers. "Might I have this dance, milady?" He didn't wait for my response, which was a stammered "not bloody likely," before we set off in a roaring, diving, circling movement that only vaguely resembled dancing.

In order to prevent my feet being trampled by his workboots-by-weekday–*slash*–armour-by-weekend, I had to move quickly to keep up, staying light and agile on my feet. His troupe, if that was what you called them, were hooting and shouting, and the audience widened into a circle to give us room.

I was completely horrified. I was a terrible dancer at the best of times, and nothing made dancing worse than public scrutiny. I could see that Micah was again dancing with one of the other lads, and she seemed to be having fun, her head back and laughing.

As for Ivan and me, we whizzed around and somehow managed to avoid major collision with anyone else. At one point, Ivan slammed his body into my chest. It seemed shockingly familiar and awfully painful given my recent contact from Rosie and her elfin sledgehammer.

"You are intoxicating, milady, as always." Ivan smiled.

"Thanks for the compliment." I responded. "I've not heard that particular one before." I jumped, trying to prevent my toes being crunched by his boots. "Don't you have a mission or something?"

"My mission is to find a fine woman to tend my hearth, warm my blankets, and bear my children." He looked at me knowingly. Oh dear. Maybe larp really was just a cover for a giant orgy?

A little put off, I shouted up at him, "I mean in the game!"

Ivan stopped dancing mid-stride. "If I didn't know your sweet nature better, I would think you were a spy." He tightened his grip on both my wrist and my waist and gave me a look of warning.

My NPC wristband was exposed and I looked over at it as a reminder.

Ivan smiled. "But of course I know your nature."

Shouts and hollers erupted. Looking over, I saw Micah kissing her dancing partner. If that was what Ivan expected, he was sorely mistaken.

"Adieu, Mr Wanderer!" I squirmed out of his grasp and made a quick exit, waving my wildflowers in the air. Micah came up for breath and quickly caught up as the crowd jeered and tried to call us back. We managed to make our way into the woods, and I, for one, was relieved no one followed.

The sun was slowly setting along the prairie horizon. Although we were headed towards the longest days of the year, the tall pine trees grew thick around us and their overhead branches effectively blocked the sun's setting rays. What light did filter through made ethereal shadows through the trunks and foliage. It was beautiful and mysterious, and I wondered what we'd find.

Chapter Twenty-Two

Walking through the woods, I couldn't help but second-guess myself. I'd been with Ralph a third of my life; was I really creeping through the forest in an attempt to spy on him? Shouldn't I just come right out and ask him for the truth?

Instead, I'd acquired an accomplice. But how else was I going to navigate this silly game? It was like travelling in a foreign country, and Micah was my tour guide. I'd still have to make the tough decisions myself, though: would I see the Roman Forum or the Coliseum?

"Micah, I really appreciate your helping me out. You didn't even know me before today."

"It's no problem. It's kind of like our own little adventure, the way I see it. A game within a game." She cleared her throat. "Well, I guess you have a little more hanging on it than just adventure. Sorry about that."

"It's not your fault." I knew I should have turned back then. Got in my car and driven back to the city. "The more I think about it, the more I wonder if maybe I overreacted. I have male friends. At work. I sometimes walk with them, we eat lunch together, it's no big deal. I'm kind of feeling a little silly now. I wonder if we should just go back and forget this." I stopped walking, and after a few paces walking on her own, Micah stopped too. She turned around, but I didn't have much more to say.

She put her hands on her hips. "You have guy friends at work. Sure. Are they secrets from Ralph? Do you spend weekends away from home and not ever mention to Ralph that you spent the whole time with a particular friend who is male?"

I threw my own hands in the air and whisper-hissed, "I thought you said they weren't having an affair! I thought you said they were probably just staying in character!"

"I said 'they might not be having an affair.'"

In the silence between us, I heard a bird calling, but nothing else. The silence stretched. I was the first to break it. "So what should I do?"

Micah, as though she were the older, more experienced one, walked over and linked her arm through mine. "Come on. We are going to that camp and we are going to watch. We might see them, we might not. You might find out what is really going on, you might not. But why not continue? You have nothing to lose. And besides," she wrinkled her nose, "that guy I was dancing with had a serious body odour issue, so do me a favour and don't make us go back that way for a little while."

We marched on.

It wasn't hard to find headquarters, even with the setting sun. We followed the trail, and once we got close to the lip of the ravine, we had a good view of the activity in the valley due to a roaring campfire. This time, I took a good look around for elves. My chest was likely bruised; it was amazing such a frail lady could hit that hard with a foam sledgehammer.

Micah found a place for us to hide behind an outcropping of rocks. We hunched down amid the grasses and weeds and tried to get as comfortable as possible.

"What's that?" I asked. Micah had taken a short cylinder out from her bodice, and I half hoped it was liquor.

"A telescope, of course."

"Right. It's lucky you brought it this weekend."

"Actually, I borrowed it."

"From who?"

"That guy with the body odour. I'll have to return it before he notices it's missing."

Jeez, I had partnered with a thief. But it was handy, no denying that.

"Okay, Gillian, take a look through this end. Rotating

this section will make it clearer. If you spot your husband or this colleague of yours, point them out to me."

Resting the lens on the back of the boulder, I studied the players in the camp. There were about fifteen mingling about, and they were mostly men. Everyone was wearing red, so I assumed they must be on the same team as Lauren. What had Margaret said while we were peeling potatoes? I couldn't remember.

"No sign of Ralph," I whispered to Micah. In fact, there was no sign of anyone in forest green with a rearing horse insignia. "What team are Ivan and his buddies on, do you think?" They didn't seem to have either crest anywhere on their armour.

"They're mercenaries. They work for whatever group pays the most."

I moved my eye away from the lens to look at her. "How do you know this shit, anyway?"

"I researched it before coming. Didn't you?"

"No. I didn't know I would need to." Looking back through the lens, I continued scanning the players. "Wait! Coming out of that tent." I pointed to the far left of the site. "Lauren. With the cape." I handed the telescope to Micah.

Micah knelt beside me and took over surveillance. Good God, I really needed a glass of wine for this. Instead, I took out my cellphone, which I still had stuffed in my own bodice. Two bars of reception! Probably a result of being on higher ground. I double-checked it was on silent mode and then thumbed out a quick text to Jas:

Am currently hiding in woods, spying on my own husband with a stolen telescope.

I pictured my friend out at a movie, reading a good book, helping her parents, or even possibly on a date with yoga man. What were the chances she'd actually see this text anytime soon? But, thankfully, her reply was almost instantaneous.

Why??

I think he might be involved with someone.

WHAT???? Are you sure?

Yes. No. Not entirely, I mean. Maybe.

Why not talk to him?

That doesn't work. Not for us.

"Hey, is that a phone?" I looked up to see Micah staring.

I shrugged. I glanced around to ensure I wasn't 'contaminating' anyone else's larp experience, but it was only us. "Sorry?" I offered.

Micah frowned but let it go. "Okay, I've spotted her too. Blonde hair, a few years younger than you, right?"

My turn to frown. "Thanks, Micah."

"I'm just making sure I've got the right person. Age isn't everything. Anyway, look at her body type. Not everyone is into that, you know."

"Right." I nodded. "There are tonnes of guys who don't like tall, thin, curvaceous women. I'll keep that in mind."

My sarcasm wasn't lost on Micah. "You're tall."

"Right." Definitely time to change the subject. "So, what's the plan?"

"I haven't seen anyone in green, so maybe your husband isn't there. For now, Lauren's walking around and talking to the other members of her army. She seems to be in charge or high ranking."

"How do you know?"

"People are saluting and deferring to her when she walks up to them." Micah went back to the spyglass, and I took the opportunity for one last illicit glance at my phone. Another text had come in from Jas.

Would you consider coming home?

Would I?

I'm staying. I'm finding out what's going on.

I stuffed my cellphone back into my corset, and Micah handed me the telescope. "Okay, I'm going in." She stood up and dusted off her skirt.

"What?" This was the plan?

"There's only so much I can find out from here to help you. I'm going to walk into the camp. Identify myself as an NPC from the kitchen and ask if they need any supplies brought in."

Micah took off without a backwards glance, and I watched her traverse the steep descent and enter the camp. Two soldiers stopped her for questioning. She showed them her wristband and they backed off. Next, she proceeded over to the campfire, where many of the players had gathered, including Lauren.

As Micah chatted with the players, I surveyed the rest of the camp. I still couldn't see Ralph. I looked at the tent I'd seen Ralph enter this afternoon. One man sat in front of the tent, but otherwise it appeared deserted. Could there be clues inside? Maybe I would find his sleeping bag. Maybe I would find evidence that a group of people were sleeping there. Or maybe just two.

The longer Micah took, the more often my gaze darted back to that tent. It didn't seem that Micah had a problem entering the camp. Maybe I would go in too. And then, as if it were a sign, the soldier deserted his post. He walked several paces and turned his back as if to urinate. This was my chance. I'd just take a quick look and then come right back to our surveillance spot.

It didn't seem risky at all.

Chapter Twenty-Three

My heart raced as I walked down the hill. I rubbed my sweaty palms on the homespun of my cloak. I didn't know how long it would take that guard to wiz. Could I make it to the tent before he returned to his post? And if I couldn't, was there any way I could still wrangle myself a peek inside the tent?

The two armoured guards who'd questioned Micah stood at the bottom of the hill, their chests stamped with the spider insignia. They raised their spears to block my path, and I waved my NPC wristband in response.

"Just checking on supplies," I said.

"Of course. Good evening, miss." The guards lowered their spears and I passed without difficulty into headquarters.

Making a direct beeline for my destination, I kept my distance from the campfire where Lauren and Micah sat. Before long I was standing in front of the tent; no one else was around. Could clues to the nature of my husband's relationship with that woman really be inside? There was only one way to find out. I took a deep breath and opened the flap.

I squinted. With the only light sources being the setting sun and the distant campfire, the contents of the tent were in shadow. It was hard to tell what I was looking at – maybe a jumble of supplies? I crawled in, and the flap dropped behind me.

It was pitch black. Reaching my hands out in front of me, I patted the ground in an attempt to feel anything recognizable, but I was fumbling over empty space. I contemplated pulling my cellphone out and using its light in my search. But my hand suddenly found something solid to grasp. It was rounded at the tip, laces on top. A work-boot? I squeezed, and suddenly it moved of its own accord.

I immediately let go. "Oh! Excuse me! I didn't realise anyone was in here." Had the guard returned and gone into the tent? What was he guarding, anyway?

I scurried back on my hands and knees towards the exit.

"Who is that?" a voice in the darkness asked. A voice I didn't need light in order to recognise.

I stopped backing up. "Ralph? Is that you?"

An awkward pause ensued. "Gillian?" His voice was incredulous. "What are you doing here?"

"What am I doing here? What are you doing in this tent?" I retorted. "Are you alone?"

"I'm larping, for God's sake. And what's that supposed to mean? Of course I'm alone."

I'd imagined this scene a thousand ways since Torres had convinced me to come on this ridiculous expedition. But I hadn't once imagined it unfolding this way. I crawled back towards Ralph, my eyes slowly adjusting to the dim light. A stool seemed to be opposite from where Ralph sat. I sat on top of it, catching my breath and trying to regain my thoughts. Although I had no answers, a wave of relief washed over me. The ruse, at least, was up.

In the silence that stretched between us, I could hear the other players at headquarters. Laughing, talking, and hanging out around the fire. It occurred to me that it was strange, Ralph sitting alone in this tent, and I wondered why he was in here rather than out there. But the moment was so surreal, I didn't give it anything but a passing thought. Here we were, only an hour from the city, completely surrounded by a fictional setting, fictional characters, fictional time zone.

Ralph was the first to speak. "I'm sorry. I didn't mean to yell. You've just completely taken me off guard." He repeated his question. "What on earth are you doing here?"

Although "spying on you" was on the tip of my tongue, it seemed perhaps a poor choice to start this conversation.

142

Instead, I went with a safer choice.

"Volunteering in the kitchens." *Good job, Gill. Now had that been hard?* "I'm an NPC." I said the initials with a small amount of pride. There. I knew more about this hobby of his than he realised.

I could hear, but still not quite see, Ralph moving around in his armour so that he faced me. "Why didn't you tell me you were coming?"

Yesterday I might have said something like "I wanted to surprise you" or "I didn't know how to tell you." But the situation had changed for me since I'd seen him with Lauren. If I'd told him I was coming...well, I'd never have witnessed the dynamics between them. I settled on another safe answer, if a bit petulant.

"I don't know."

Ralph didn't ask me to elaborate. "Are you having fun?"

"This whole thing is...weird. Kind of trippy. I wasn't exactly sure what to expect, but it's not as bad as I feared. Some people are actually quite normal." I smiled, thinking of Micah and Margaret.

"I like how you can just completely forget about all your real problems," said Ralph. "When you're in game, you can just immerse yourself in the story, and that's all that matters."

"But do you know what gets to me, Ralph? It's pretend."

Ralph's comments had triggered my annoyance. In the twenty-four hours I'd been there, I hadn't for once forgotten my real problems. And I'd come so ridiculously far, sitting in the middle of the wilderness in wench wear. Unsure how long we'd have before being interrupted, I pushed forward.

"It seems like you'd rather play pretend than spend time with me. Your wife." I could feel the emotion make my heart race and my fingers shake. "Ralph, do you have something to tell me?"

"Tell you?"

I didn't bother answering his stall tactic. I would wait him out.

"Are you serious?" Instead of sounding contrite, Ralph's

voice was decidedly defensive. "You came all the way out here to have the same damn fight we always have? What's wrong with you?"

Suddenly, sounds from outside the tent intensified. The quiet conversations and ramblings of camp life were overpowered by shouting.

"Does anyone know you're here?" Ralph asked.

"I told Jas."

"I meant *in game*. Does anyone know you're in this tent?"

In the dark, I rolled my eyes. "Who cares? You haven't answered my question yet. Do you have something to tell me?"

"What are you getting at?" Ralph seemed only half in the conversation. Although my eyes had adjusted somewhat to the darkness, I couldn't see his face clearly. I could, however, see his body turn first to the left, then the right, trying to figure out what was causing the commotion outside the tent. He was still more concerned about this game than me.

"I saw you today, Ralph." I took a deep breath to steady my voice. "I saw you enter this tent, and I saw you at breakfast. Is there something you want to tell me? Something you owe me?"

"What does that mean?"

"I saw you, Ralph! You were with Lauren."

"And?" Was he being obtuse on purpose? "What are you trying to accuse me of, Gillian?"

"You've never once told me that you hang out with her at these things. And it certainly makes me curious about what you're hiding. Because normally if you saw someone I knew, you might say something like 'Oh, Gillian, I saw Lauren at the grocery store today. She says hi.'"

"This isn't the grocery store, Gill."

"It makes no difference!" I slammed my hands down on my homespun-covered knees.

Ralph resorted to his favourite communication tool. Silence. Which just made me feel irrational and reactionary.

I knew what I'd seen.

But after several stormy breaths, Ralph caved. "There are game rules here, Gill. You've got to stay in character at all times. Even if you know someone from outside the game, you never acknowledge that relationship because it kind of ruins the game. Besides, you aren't interested in what happens here, so why would I tell you?"

"You're being paternalistic and shitty. You don't need to explain your hobby to me as though I were a child." My voice was rising. Ralph held a hand up to me, indicating I should be silent, and turned his head towards the tent entrance. I didn't care. "Just tell me the truth. Did you sleep with that woman?"

Ralph's body flinched. He turned his head back towards me, and I was glad I couldn't actually see his eyes, his expression. "This isn't real life, Gill, it's a game. Would you stop and think what you're saying for a minute?"

"What do you mean by that? Are you trying to insinuate that if you sleep with someone *in game* it's not a real affair? You don't think it counts?"

I could have continued with my ranting, rasping, and death-threat whispering, but to my horror, I could feel tears welling at the corner of my eyes and I blinked furiously, refusing to let them fall. Even though Ralph wouldn't be able to see me, he'd be able to hear the incredibly large ball of emotion that was forming in my throat, threatening to choke me on every word I tried to say. This was perhaps the moment that would end my marriage, and I needed to be strong. To hold on to whatever dignity I had left.

It took Ralph a while to respond. A while of staring through the dark at each other, each willing the other to do something so rash they could be excused for hammering the other to death with a larp broadsword or boffer. Well, I was, at least.

"It means I'm not an idiot. I know the difference between real life and a game. And you better goddamn well believe that I save the things that matter for real life. So, no, Gill, I did not 'sleep with that woman'...but have I wanted to? To be with someone who wasn't fighting me all the time? To have sex with someone who could laugh and have fun and shows a shred of interest? Well, yes, Gill. Yes, I've damn well wanted to."

A million ideas flew haphazard in my head, but not one slowed long enough for me to catch it. I felt small. And tired. I didn't know if this was worse than an actual affair. To hear him admit there were more attractive people, more enjoyable people out there. Disloyal, perhaps. But not a lie. And not the kind of thing Ralph and I had ever admitted before.

A thought finally slowed enough to flutter down from my tornado mind, settling into my numb heart. Our life together had become one unending fight. For Ralph to find happiness elsewhere, no matter how fictional, was human. Natural. Inevitable.

"You coming out here, not telling me, spying or something, and drawing your own inane conclusions. It sounds an awful lot like you don't trust me," Ralph said.

"If the shoe fucking fits!" It was sometimes hard to remember that you weren't alone when you were sitting in a dark tent with just one other person. I don't know why I was so surprised when the tent flap opened and a kerosene lamp popped in accompanied by a rather young and sparsely whiskered face.

"What's going on here?"

I squinted against the sudden light, holding up my wristband. I could go anywhere, right?

His head popped back out and he called, "Zienna! Prisoner tent!"

Inside the tent, Ralph leaned towards me. I couldn't see his face, but I could hear the anger in his voice. "So you didn't trust me? You came out here not to support me, but to spy on me? Because you didn't trust me?" He sounded furious. Well, good.

"I don't know, Ralph," I hissed back. "Should I trust you?" I was angry. And wounded. He'd told me his feelings, and I knew in my gut that he'd given an honest answer.

How had I ended up in this big production, anyway? This whole thing – Torres's great idea about taking an interest in Ralph's hobby as a way of building quality time into our relationship – had completely backfired. I should've told him I was coming. I'd known it, I just hadn't done it. But that was about all I had time to register before the kerosene lamp was back.

And this time, it was accompanied by a scarlet cape, a spider insignia, and long blonde hair.

Chapter Twenty-Four

Lauren and I made eye contact and held it, both of us squinting in the light. My face flushed with shame, reliving what Ralph had admitted. I couldn't help but notice how soft her skin was, how young her face. Her long tousled hair glistened in the light, and I swallowed my jealousy. Yes, she was a beautiful woman, but my husband was not having an affair with her. Yet. I would not be a crazy, bitter wife. I would instead handle this incredibly awkward situation with wit and maturity.

"Hi there," I said in greeting.

She turned towards the pimply guard who was now also crawling into the tent. "Leave us," she said. He obeyed immediately, and she took a seat on a box by the tent entrance, then placed the lamp down on the ground between us.

It was then I noticed that Ralph's hands were bound with rope. Why was he being held here? Was *he* the prisoner?

"Are you a spy?" Her tone was terse, rigid.

"Ah, no. I'm a French horn player. Same as last week." I smiled. Who could play this game with a straight face, anyway?

"Pardon me?" Apparently, she could.

"French horn. You know, large lumbering instrument that keeps you flighty woodwinds from racing about." Neither Ralph nor Lauren looked impressed with my wit.

"Is this some kind of code language? Are you trying to broker a deal with me, the leader of Arachne's Army, for the life of this prisoner? Or should I take you for a halfwit?" She sneered.

Yes, my chin dropped. I looked over at Ralph, but his

face was blank. The three of us obviously knew each other. Were we really going to sit around in a tent and pretend we didn't? This was not sane.

"Look." I lifted my arm to revel my NPC wristband. "I'm helping out in the kitchens and just came down here to…chat."

Her eyes darted between Ralph and me before she folded her arms across her chest and laughed. "How sweet. The great warrior knight has a wench slaving away in the kitchens. Tending his fire and warming his bed."

Jumping to my feet, my head crashed into the canvas roof of the goddamn tent, taking what little dignity I had left and destroying it.

"Excuse me?" I patted my hair back as best I could and then balled my hands into fists by my sides. My face was hot with embarrassment, but I could do nothing but push on. I wasn't going to allow her to throw me under the medieval bus. I had the sudden urge to grab one of the brown felt magic bags hanging from her belt and throw it in her face, but a voice behind me spoke before I could do anything.

"I do not know this woman." It was cold and short, and it was Ralph's.

Obviously, they were both determined to stay in game character, but I felt personally rejected anyway. And dumb. Ralph had once again chosen this game over me.

I wasn't sure what to do. I was standing, they were sitting. Lauren looked from Ralph to me, then back to Ralph. Ralph himself looked down at his feet, not making eye contact with either of us.

"If that's the case," I said, trying to rouse as much authority as I could find, "I'll just be going, then." I tugged on the bottom of my leather bodice for lack of something better to do with my hands. "Have yourselves a blast sitting in this tent all weekend. Sure seems like a hell of a lot of fun."

I started to edge around Lauren, but she put her hand up, palm facing me. "You aren't going anywhere until you've been interrogated. I will not have you spread secrets to the

149

enemy."

"Right. Because I so care about your stupid little game."

Still, Ralph didn't say anything.

I heard voices and people outside the tent, and so did Lauren. Turning around, she backed up as someone new entered the tent. It was going to be stifling in here with all these people, and I certainly hoped the kerosene lamp didn't get knocked over. Why would people ever turn their back on a good, simple and safe flashlight? It was beyond me.

Coarse brown hair appeared, followed by a thick beard, armoured shoulders, and then the rest of my bulky admirer.

"Milady, what on earth are you doing here? You sure do…get around! And all along you've been playing shy with the sheets!" Dear God, could this situation get worse? "Perhaps you are…available?"

"I am not chattel, to be traded from man to man. But yes, Ivan, perhaps I am available!" I was so mad at Ralph, I wanted to kick him with the heel of my boot in the shin, but I desisted.

No one knew that Ralph and I had just had one of the worst conversations of our marriage. That it didn't even seem clear what the future held for us. What I did know was that he was as unhappy as I was. And now we were stuck with a tent full of strangers, fumbling around in costumes in the middle of the woods.

"Ivan, oh, Great Wanderer, have you by chance happened upon my friend?" I said this in a stilted voice, to be sure, but it was the best I could manage at present.

"That wee minx Thomas is fond of? She has headed back to the kitchen to inquire for help releasing you from Arachne's Army—"

"Tie her up, Ivan," said Lauren. "You are paid to do my bidding, not to flirt with my prisoners." And with that, she headed out of the tent.

"You've got to be kidding!" I yelled as she crawled out of the tent. "I'm a volunteer, for crying out loud!"

Ivan tied my hands and left me alone in the tent with Ralph. He left the kerosene lamp, and I wasn't sure I didn't prefer the darkness.

For a long time neither of us spoke. What was there left to say, anyway? But I found something, of course. "Thanks for totally humiliating me there, Ralph. That was great."

He looked up at me. "Did you read the rules before you signed up to spy on me?"

I rolled my eyes. Wow. He was really sensitive about this. "I don't know, Ralph. Did you read the rules before you signed up to marry me?"

"NPCs cannot interfere with the game."

"For richer or poorer! For better or worse!" I swallowed before adding in a calmer voice, "Besides, I'm allowed to walk around the camp. That's why they give you these wristbands."

"Sure. But that doesn't include going rogue, entering people's tents and stopping prisoners from being rescued, which would allow the game to continue. Do you know how many people paid money to enact this scene this weekend?"

My turn to be silent. See how he liked it.

Oh, forget it, I'm crap at that. "You care more about this stupid game than saving our marriage!" I shot the words across the tent at him. "I'm trying everything, and you do nothing but entertain yourself with dumb games!"

"And you think spying on me and accusing me of having an affair is helpful at all?" He shot the words right back. "You are very self-righteous."

My stomach fell to somewhere deep in my pelvic floor, leaving an empty space to allow my heart to slip into the bitter spot where my liver used to reside. I could hear movement and voices outside, and they seemed to be coming towards the tent. It was now or never.

"Maybe I didn't do it right, but I tried. I came here. I got this ridiculous outfit, I figured out how to volunteer, and I came out here. I'm seeing a therapist, Ralph. Because I care about this marriage. And now look. I'm sitting in this tent. Wearing ridiculous clothes, feeling stupid and out of place. And please tell me, what have you done? Are you doing anything to help this marriage?"

I clenched the fabric of my cloak in my fists. The words had been a hot flame on my tongue, and I was glad to be rid of them. Leaning forward, feeling hurt and angry in equal parts, I spat, "You stay married to me because you are too weak to leave. But the truth is, you'd rather be anywhere as long as it's not with me."

Our eyes locked in the light of the kerosene lamp, and I dearly hoped the lamp did not tip over. I had now balled up my cloak so tightly there was no extra fabric to squeeze. The thought came to me that it was either rip it in two, destroying it, or let go and be done with it.

It was infuriating that I couldn't get up and leave.

Ralph sighed. "Yes, Gill. You've done all these things." He lifted his tied hands and rubbed his forehead before letting them fall back to his lap. "But you've skipped the most important thing, don't you think?"

Rather than answer, I focused on my breathing, willing myself not to cry.

"You've never faced it, Gill. That we lost him. You act like it didn't happen. But it did. It changed you. You're stuck in this pattern of focusing on everything else but what happened. And no amount of custom cabinetry or weekends together or even counselling will change the past. I'm not an expert. But it seems to me you can't move forward if you haven't grieved.

"And it definitely changed me too. And so, yes, you're right. I'd rather pretend out here, in this fake universe, than be home pretending the most important thing in our lives never happened."

Although Ralph's tone was calm, his words hit me like a wave of salt water, pushing my body back with a cold slap, stinging my eyes and lips. It was the worst kind of pain to not be able to walk away. To know the truth and stare it back in the face.

But that's what I did. Until, finally, someone returned to the tent.

"Gretchen, my sweet," Ivan said, "I have brought you your champion."

Margaret scrambled into the tent and started untying my wrists, explaining in a loud voice to whoever was within earshot that I was very new to the village and just learning how to earn my keep. I was a halfwit besides, known to wander and generally speak nonsense. She led me out of the tent and I followed.

I did not say goodbye.

Chapter Twenty-Five

We started back to the refuge of our volunteer dorm. Micah held the kerosene lamp, which had been graciously lent to help us through the now-dark forest. Our progress was slow, but thankfully no sledgehammers attacked us. I waited until after we climbed the steep path leading out of the ravine before speaking.

"Thanks, Margaret, for, you know, the village idiot thing."

"Don't thank me, thank Micah. She came and got me as soon as she realised you had involved yourself in gameplay. You've got to stay in character at all times when you're out here. And you can't be changing the course of play. If you want to do that, you've got to sign up as a player character next time, okay?"

"It's okay, Margaret. I don't think there will be a next time. I'm sorry if I caused trouble." Sure enough, behind us in the distance I could hear the sounds of a battle erupting back at headquarters. It was a little embarrassing that I had held up all these people, and I hoped everyone didn't know it had been Ralph's cracked wife's fault. Had they been hiding in the woods all this time?

"Didn't you have fun?" Margaret sounded a little saddened.

"Oh, it's not that... I met lots of lovely people. Especially in the kitchen. It's just...I'm having a bit of a personal issue." My throat caught, and I tried to cover it by coughing.

"What an asshole!" Micah seethed. "Did he deny it?"

"Oh...I think maybe I was wrong."

Margaret didn't ask, and I was hoping Micah wouldn't

continue, but no luck. "And you believed him? The cheating bastard! We should've roasted his balls, Margaret!"

I held up my hands. "No, no. I really think I may have overreacted. Imagination, you know." In the dim light, I could see Margaret and Micah look from me to each other.

Margaret put her arm around me, and we started walking again. "It's okay. It's your story, and you don't have to tell us if you don't want to." She gave Micah a firm look and we continued walking.

"What a douche," Micah mumbled under her breath.

"It's complicated, Micah. Marriage." We kept walking through the woods, each in our own thoughts. I had been sure I wanted a way out. I had that now. Not because he was having an affair, but because it was obvious to both of us that there was nothing left.

I didn't feel excited about freedom. I felt like a pile of dog shit on a hot day.

Sleep would not come easily for the second night in a row. I felt sick with doubt and shame at my behaviour in the tent. And the old taste of grief was silver in my mouth.

What did Ralph know, anyway? He said I needed to grieve, but of course I had grieved. Every damn day. '*You can't move on if you don't grieve*,' he'd said. As though moving on was something I'd want to do.

Perhaps it was easier for Ralph – he hadn't felt a baby move within his body. He hadn't lain awake in the wee hours as a child danced the rumba in his belly. But I had. I had known morning sickness. I had tasted the anticipation of growing too round for even your most forgiving clothing. The swollen ankles, the sacrifices of wine, caffeine, and unpasteurised cheese for weeks on end.

But we had both shared the ultrasound appointment. The anticipation of those first glimpses of a child – grey and white and murky – had somehow made it more real. More permanent than a second pink line on a stick. I couldn't wait to see the shape of our child's skull, the outline of a snub nose or spider-thin fingers.

I'd booked the appointment on a day without rehearsals with the orchestra, and Ralph had taken the afternoon off work. We'd met, as planned, at the coffee shop down the street from the technician's lab. I'd ordered the ginger tea to settle my oft-queasy stomach. I never drink it now. Even the smell of that tea sends me back to those treasured early weeks filled with mystery and anticipation.

By the time we got to the lab, my bladder was pressing urgently for release. But I was a first-time-mother rule follower: I'd been warned that the technician would need me to have a full bladder in order to take the best images, so I'd drunk the recommended amount of water before leaving the house. I'd already planned to order the digital images. To print off the pictures and send them to our family back in Ontario.

We sat on a bench in the private change room, waiting to be called in by the ultrasound tech. Me in a paper gown and underwear, Ralph anxiously holding my folded clothes and purse. I regretted the extra tea. My bladder was bursting.

I turned to Ralph, taking in his bouncing knee and ruddy complexion. "Do you think it might be a girl?"

"Maybe. Are you really sure you want to find out?"

I smiled and squeezed his soon-to-be-an-adoring-father hand. I loved this man. Couldn't imagine life without him. "If you're still dead set on a surprise, then we can wait. It's only five more months. That's just twenty-two long weeks of not knowing…"

"You're right." Ralph laughed. He could barely keep birthday presents a secret. "Let's find out."

It was our first glimpse at our future, and we couldn't wait. Sitting there in that crinkling paper shirt, holding my pee, I knew only excitement. I was flush with it.

"I hope she'll have your curly hair." Ralph wrapped one of my brown loopy curls around his finger.

"I hope he won't get stuck with your knobbly elbows."

We giggled and held hands, anticipating the beauty of our child's fingers, the ten precious toes, the perfectly formed body.

We'd never heard the words *trisomy eighteen* before. I'd only just read the term on the pamphlet given to me when I booked the ultrasound. It wasn't Down syndrome; wasn't anything like it. Because this trisomy was considered *not compatible with life*.

But it never happened. Not to people you actually knew. The probability was like one in a million. Or, as it turns out, one in five thousand.

And someone has to be that one.

I rolled over in my bunk. My feet were freezing in the bottom of the womb-like sleeping bag. Which was appropriate, the way I saw it. Wombs, regardless of what people wanted to believe, did not ensure safety. They didn't ensure anything.

Ralph

My blasted back was agony. Spending hours with my hands tied together, hadn't allowed me to stretch properly. And now, lying in my down-filled sleeping bag on top of the hard earth, I was desperate for a muscle relaxant or two. The cold seeped up through the ground and so did the sharp rocks. I rolled onto my side, trying to find some level of comfort, but it was pointless.

Even if I could find some physical comfort, my mind was too active to sleep. But I seemed to be the only one having trouble; the grunts, farts and snores of my compatriots were evidence enough that everyone else in our tent was sleeping. We shared it, this tent. Four of us Horsemen had invested in the dark green canvas, and I'd never had trouble sleeping in it till now.

The weekend had started out fine. My role had been pretty clear: The Gamesmaster had assigned me the job of Horseman diplomat. My mission was to portray a convincing representative looking to broker a deal with Arachne's Army. But my true task had been to act as a distraction. The rest of my crew were planning a surprise raid at twilight on Arachne's headquarters, and our chances of success were better if our enemy thought the Horseman were seeking peace.

And so, I'd spent practically the entire day in diplomatic duties, being entertained by the Arachne mistress Zienna. Until some elf alerted her army to my dual purpose.

Sitting in a supply tent, hands tied together: not so fun. And then, of course, as the day had turned into night, it had rolled into a downright disaster.

I signed. Damn it, Gillian. I had been shocked to see her.

Our conversation had digressed into a useless argument with reckless speed. I already regretted the way I'd handled the situation.

I didn't regret anything I'd said. No. I'd needed to say those things, and I was pretty sure Gillian had needed to be straight with me too. But it was how we'd said it. Why were we so damn bad at saying the important stuff nicely?

I wondered if my wife were sleeping, or if she was also replaying the night's events the same as I was. Without a doubt, I knew she would be hurting. She'd been hurting for a long time.

Gillian changed in an instant. It's just I'd been too much of a dumbass to understand how permanent the change would be until much later. I should have known it, the moment we'd found out about our child's condition. And if not, then the meeting with the genetic counsellor should have alerted me. The doctor had even spelled it out for us, what our son's condition meant in very practical terms. How fleeting our time with him would be – if, in fact, we would have any.

Yes, Gillian had said. Her eyes glassy, her gaze focused on something I couldn't see. She'd understood. We'd both understood.

Her tummy grew and I'd see her hand on her abdomen, counting the movements. His elbows shoving and feet restlessly dancing against her ribcage. This life – so palpable, so active – and yet it wasn't to be.

It was hard to reconcile.

Gillian stopped going to the mall. She stopped doing the grocery shopping. She turned away when people asked when she was due and didn't respond to them. Not that I blamed her. That she was expecting became obvious. But what we were expecting – a loss rather than a life – was not so obvious.

I saw the pain in her eyes when these questions came up. And yes, I suggested it one night. The possibility given us by the medical team. It was a solution, wasn't it? We knew the outcome already. Was there any point to continuing this mental suffering? It was unnecessary torture, I'd reasoned.

Gillian looked at me through the haze that had settled in her eyes. I can remember the look she'd given me. It wasn't anger, or frustration or sadness. She was puzzled. It was as though she didn't know who I was, or perhaps how I could think or feel something so different from her.

Against the odds Gillian carried our child to term. And again, against the odds, he'd lived. For two hours, he had lived. For me, what had previously been a condition – a predetermined luck-of-the-draw statistic – had become our beautiful child. The beautiful child Gillian had waited for all along.

We'd taken turns holding him. Our son. Gillian's arms were greedy for whatever time she had, and not wanting to steal that from her, I had passed our son back long before I was ready to let him go. We stayed together as his breathing slowed. The space between his inhalations widening, until finally, peacefully, he drew his last.

It wasn't until I found the little cupboard back at home. The one filled with soft, folded cotton in patterns of blue giraffes and green and yellow strips. The pyjamas Gillian had stored away, the ones with the buttons down the front and the feet attached. That's when I realised. She'd held out hope against the odds.

I rolled over, still trying for comfort as a cold wind blew through our canvas tent. The rhythmic sound of snoring surrounded me, inviting me into slumber. But sleep would not come.

Chapter Twenty-Six

The next morning I was back on the porridge cauldron. Funny, it was less than forty-eight hours later, but I felt a weird sense of nostalgia about leaving. Maybe because I'd met some very supportive folks. And maybe because I knew there was no going back to what had been life...before larp. My marriage had reached the pathetic state of being measurable in pre-larp and post-larp terms.

"You okay?" Micah was standing beside me in a flowing soft green gown that showed a fair amount of cleavage for this early in the morning. I didn't think I was the only one who noticed.

"Sure. Just feel a bit like a house-cat who ate a pile of rat poison. Nothing that won't wear off...eventually."

Micah looked at me strangely, and I didn't blame her. Even though I'd said it, I couldn't really explain exactly what I meant. Other than very shitty. Might as well change the subject.

"I saw you slip out of the bunkhouse pretty late last night." I gave Micah a sidelong glance. I'd eventually fallen asleep only to slip in and out of strange dreams, and although I'd seen her leave, I had no idea when or if she'd made it back to our dorm.

Micah flushed. She waited until there was a gap in porridge patrons to answer. "I ended up hooking up with one of the guys from last night."

My eyebrows shot up. "The one who stank?"

Micah gave me a look of disgust. "Not him! Are you kidding? The tall one. Blond hair. Moustache."

Oh. Dear. Really? She was referring to the guard at the tent in headquarters. With the sparse facial hair and the slightly pimpled complexion. I wondered if he had tried growing the moustache for his larp character or if he sported it on a regular basis.

"Oh. Well, he certainly is….tall. And polite." In all honesty, I hadn't really noticed much else about him because I'd been so focused on my personal crisis. "What's he like?"

"He's really kind." She gushed. "Of course I don't really know a lot about him. He's one of those who like to stay in character at all times. I hope he actually lives in the city! But he is very complementary and very sweet, and his body isn't half-bad either." She elbowed me in the ribs, and I smiled.

"Sounds like all the makings of a fine relationship." I didn't think it was necessary to crush her with the reality of common interests, compatible spending habits, gender roles, life goals, and the like. She had plenty of time for all that. "Seriously, I'm happy for you. But what are you going to do now? Wait outside the campground to exchange modern day contact information?"

"Oh, I gave him my number already. Explained it was a coded message with magical potential, and he pocketed it immediately."

"Ha! You are a smart cookie, Micah."

I looked up and there, at the end of our porridge line, was Ralph. Today he was with a small group of like-dressed individuals. I took this to mean he'd been successfully rescued by the Horsemen's Army. I wanted desperately to leave. To march back into the kitchen and not have to face him in the light. But what was the point? Everything was on the table, with nothing left to hide.

Micah sensed my tension, and we served on in semi-silence.

Finally, it was Ralph's turn, and we served him like any other. If he wanted to stay in character, I would also. I didn't make eye contact, I just kept about my work. He hesitated before leaving as though he wanted to say something. But I turned and started serving the man behind him, and he could do nothing but move forward.

After breakfast was over and the kitchen volunteers had eaten together and cleaned up, I exchanged hugs and contact information with Micah before seeking out Margaret.

"Thank you for all your help," I said in farewell.

"It was very nice meeting you, Gillian. I hope you come back."

A wave of wistfulness washed over me again. I had learned that this place wasn't as full of weirdos as I had thought. But I wasn't coming back. There would be no point.

We hugged, and she whispered in my ear, "Good luck. I know it's tough, but you never know. There is always hope... Life can surprise us sometimes."

I blinked furiously. My throat was too thick with emotion to respond. Yes. Life was full of surprises. I gathered my belongings and trudged up to my car.

Time for the real world.

Chapter Twenty-Seven

The real world didn't wait for me to arrive back in Calgary. It hit as soon as I was within cellular service range, even if I hadn't realised at first. That might've been for a few reasons: Although I'd powered my phone on, I'd tossed it on the passenger seat, carelessly covering it with a puddle of rented cloak. I'd then proceeded to drown myself in the tragic melodies of a rather melancholy playlist. I was taking my battered soul back to the real world, and the louder the music, the better to sob.

Just outside of city limits, I pulled off the highway at a service station. My gas tank was nearly empty, and this place seemed as good as any to fill it up. Besides, I wasn't likely to run into anyone who knew me while I was still in costume, my eyes red rimmed and puffy. Out of habit, I reached over to check my phone before getting out to pump the gas.

Three text messages from Jas had been delivered, and I hadn't heard one ping.

Dad's had a heart attack. It's bad. They're not sure he will make it.

I'm at the Peter Lougheed hospital with Mom.

Can't get a hold of Arianna – she won't respond to my texts. Had a fight last night.   Long story. Could you try? She might respond to you.

Had Jas just sent these this morning? Or had they been delayed because of the bad cellular coverage at the camp? I had no idea. While I'd been consumed with my own pitiful life, disaster had struck the Singhs.

Oh Jas. I am so sorry about your dad. And I'm on it. I'll find Arianna and get her there.

Oh man, this did not sound good. I immediately thought of poor Mrs Singh and how scared she must be. They'd been married practically her whole adult life, and I'd rarely ever seen her without him. Did she even drive? I didn't think so.

And what if Mr Singh died and Arianna didn't have a chance to say goodbye? It wouldn't be the first time she'd lost someone without being able to say farewell, and I didn't want to see it happen again. Especially if it resulted from some trivial fight with her mom. Neither would forgive themselves.

I fired a quick text to Arianna.

Honey, where are you? Call or text me ASAP!

Then another to Jas.

If she doesn't respond to my text, any ideas where else to try?

I turned my car back on, giving up on the gas. I would surely be fine without it; the light had only just come on. I must have at least fifty kilometres or so before it would actually be empty.

I keep numbers of her friends' parents in the kitchen junk drawer. Maybe she's at one of their homes?

That was quickly followed by a second text.

They are worried about the clot breaking off and causing a stroke. So scared. Mom's not good.

And, as if reading my wondering mind, a third text followed.

Caught Arianna lying about where she was. Told me she was with her girlfriend working on a school project and it turns out she was at the mall with that boy from the party.

Ahhh. Well, that answers that.

Don't worry about that now.

She quickly sent back a response.

There's nothing else to do but worry. We are stuck in a waiting room at ICU. I'm worried Dad won't make it. And... I overreacted with Arianna. Big time.

I sat staring at my phone, not sure what to say. Once again, I'd been consumed with this ridiculous larp adventure and hadn't looked past my nose at other people's concerns. Friday had offered a perfect chance for me to talk to Arianna one-on-one about that boy, and I'd chosen the easy way out and not even asked her about him. Jas had been right. I'd been keeping busy rather than dealing with what really mattered.

But I was going to get Arianna to the hospital. The clot, the past, I'd no control over any of that, but finding Arianna, I could do that. I knew she'd want to be there for her grandfather. If the worst happened and she didn't even have a chance to say goodbye.... No. I wouldn't waste more time worrying about that now. I started up my car and thumbed out a quick last reply to Jas.

I love you, honey, hold on. I'm on my way and I'll get Arianna. It's going to be...

I was going to write *okay*, but I stopped myself. Deleted

my last sentence. How many times had people given me that pat answer? And it wasn't true. Life wasn't always okay. It was life. And sometimes that meant it sucked. So that's what I finished with instead.

I'm sorry this sucks. I'm here for you.

I pressed send before ripping out of the parking lot and speeding back towards the city.

Using my Bluetooth, I tried calling Arianna three times while driving before I gave up on that tactic. No answer. On the third try, I left a voice message.

"Hi, honey. It's me, Gill. Look – I know you and your mom had an argument. I don't know anything about it, and it doesn't matter anyway. There's something a lot more important going on, and I really need you to call me back. It's important, okay?' I ended the call and gripped the steering wheel.

Five minutes more, and I was submerged in heavy traffic; I was literally surrounded by a slow crawl of city folks returning from weekend trips to the mountains. We crept along, ever closer to the city centre, but it was anything but fast. I started to worry about my rash decision not to purchase gas. Sure, I could stop at another gas station, but I didn't want to waste time. I would head to Jas and Arianna's home first and see what I could find in the junk drawer. That meant an extra twenty minutes to the suburbs. I tapped my fingers on the steering wheel, willing the traffic to move more quickly.

Thirty minutes passed, and I was still making slow progress. In all that time, Arianna didn't return my call. I wondered if she was ignoring her phone or had turned it off after several calls from her mother. Or maybe she didn't trust me and thought I was trying to trick her on behalf of her mother. Or perhaps her cell battery had simply died. That wasn't impossible, although it seemed to me that younger people would rather be caught with their pants down than be disconnected from the virtual world.

167

Oh shit. Maybe that's what had happened? She got caught with her pants down? Shit. She was only fourteen. I sped up and passed the minivan in front of me that was religiously sticking to the speed limit. Arianna was too young in my opinion – never mind her mother's – for that type of intimacy. But that was common nowadays, wasn't it? If the media could be trusted, all teenagers were doing drugs, having sex, and trying to commit suicide on practically a daily basis.

I gripped the wheel more tightly. Was there any way to keep a kid safe these days? I couldn't blame Jas for the stiff restrictions she placed on her daughter, even if I could identify with how unfair they seemed to Arianna.

But this was silly. I had no idea what they'd fought about. Arianna was a good kid. It was just a fight with her mother – she was probably interested in seeing this guy but knew she wouldn't have permission, so she likely just said she was with a girlfriend. It didn't mean they were having sex. Or smoking pot. Or contemplating death.

Regardless, I was in over my head. What would I tell her? I didn't have any authority to change the rules or enforce them – that was her mom's job. And I was woefully inexperienced in that realm. I had an errant thought to contact Micah and ask for her sidekick help again – if only it could be that easy.

But this was my job, and I'd do it. I'd find Arianna and get her where she needed to be. The list in the junk drawer would be my next strategy. I crossed my fingers, hoping my gas tank would hold out.

It did. Entering their home with my spare key, I dashed to the junk drawer and threw it open. Jas's meticulous list was easy to find – did my friend really keep even her junk drawer this neat? – a list of ten or so contacts with child's name, parent's name, address and phone number, and, occasionally, birthdates. Wow. I didn't even have a list like this for my blood relatives.

I sat down at the table and got busy phoning.

Chapter Twenty-Eight

I'd practically exhausted the phone list, leaving several awkward voice messages and participating in a few fruitless conversations, but nothing useful had yet materialised. There was only one number left to try, and I dialled it.

"Hello?" A woman's voice answered on the second ring.

I looked down at the list for the correct name. "Hi there, is this Lisa's mom? Theresa?" I managed to rush it out with barely a stammer.

Pause. I could hear the indecision in the silence. I imagined her wondering who the heck was on the other end of the line and what I was attempting to sell. "Yes, it is. May I ask who this is?"

"Oh. Yes, for sure. My name's Gillian. I'm a family friend of Arianna Barber. I'm her godmother, actually, and I'm looking for her. Her mother – Jaspreet – and I have been trying to get a hold of her all day, but she hasn't responded to her phone." I didn't want to get into specifics because I felt Arianna should know about her grandfather before her circle of friends did. "It's really important that we get a hold of Arianna right away. There's been a family emergency. Do you, by chance, know where she is?"

Again a pause. "I'm sorry, who did you say this was?" I rolled my eyes. I understood being careful with revealing personal information, but if no one was going to trust me, how was I going to find Arianna?

"Look, I'm Gillian. Gillian Campbell. I'm Arianna's godmother. Arianna's mother is in the midst of a family crisis, and Arianna is not returning her calls. We need to find her right away. Do you know where she is?"

"I don't," she said, and then added, "but let me check

with Lisa." There, finally. I just needed to be firm. Direct. Channel my inner Jas. I could hear Theresa calling her daughter but couldn't make out the hushed conversation between the two of them.

I heard a muffled sound and then Theresa was speaking back into the receiver again. "Gillian?"

"Yes?"

"We're not sure where Arianna is right now. She and Lisa were together this afternoon but parted ways a few hours ago. I picked Lisa up at the mall and Arianna was going to take the bus home. Have you tried her house?"

"I'm standing in their kitchen now. She's not here."

"Okay, I've had Lisa text Arianna and maybe we'll hear something that way."

"Thank you. That's a great idea." This mom knew what she was doing. Working through the kid. Very wise. The seconds ticked by in awkward silence, as we all waited for Lisa to receive a response to her text.

"Hello? Gillian? The Starbucks by the mall!" Theresa's voice sounded triumphant through the phone. Then I heard a muffled "Lisa! Stop right now! Do not say some lady is looking for her!"

"I'm headed right over." Looked like Arianna was simply avoiding running into her mother. I remembered doing the same to my own mother. I was going to fly in there and freak her right out.

"Oh. She's with someone, I guess…"

"A boy?" I asked.

"You got it."

"Thanks for the heads up. But, hey, how much trouble can you get into at a coffee shop?"

"You'd be surprised." Theresa's voice was grim, and I shuddered as the thought of the coffee shop's notoriously spacious bathrooms came to mind. I thanked Theresa for her time and raced back out to my car. This time I caught nearly every green light and arrived at the Starbucks in record time, my empty gas light now flashing dangerously fast.

I ripped into the parking lot – practically catching air

under my tyres as I sailed over the speed bump – and parked haphazardly in an empty spot. There she was. I could see her through the storefront window. Sitting at a table, her hands fumbling with the half-empty transparent plastic cup in front of her, she was gazing across the table at her companion. I recognised the young man immediately.

As soon as I'd pulled my key out of the ignition, I swung my car door open. I stepped my left foot out of the car when the sight of my homespun tunic around my knees stopped me in my tracks. Shit. The costume.

Oh well, this was an emergency. I got out of the car and firmly tugged the bottom edge of the corset down. I'd just have to proceed as is.

I first tried waving through the window at Arianna, hoping to get her to come to me without embarrassing her too much, but I couldn't seem to pull her attention away from young Romeo's eyes. I opened the door and walked as discreetly as possible towards the self-serve station. It happened to be directly behind the boy.

Staring over the stacks of lids and containers of cream, I finally managed to gain Arianna's attention. Her eyes widened in surprise before narrowing to slits. I motioned with my hand for her to come over to me. She glared and looked away, pretending I wasn't even there. The guy started talking again.

Right. Did she really think I would back down? Enough was enough. I'd apparently have to go in for the kill.

The barista was giving me an odd look. I wished it were closer to Halloween. But it wasn't, and we did not have time to waste. Making up my mind, I marched up to the table and pulled out a third chair that was sitting empty beside Arianna. Picking up my skirts, I sat down in a cascade of homespun and creaking leather.

"Hello." I extended my hand to the young man, who looked startled. "I'm Gillian, Arianna's godmother. We've not met properly." He looked briefly at Arianna and then back at me before extending his hand and shaking mine.

"And you are?" I prompted.

"Oh." He cleared his throat nervously. "I'm Jiwan. Nice to meet you?" His statement came out rather high-pitched, making it sound more a question than a statement.

"It is, isn't it." I smiled, still not looking at Arianna. I understood that she was upset with her mother, but I was starting to get frustrated as her anger spilled over towards me. That hadn't really happened before. I had always been the good cop while her mother, who set the rules, was bad cop. "I imagine you care about Arianna, and so I hope you understand I need to have a serious conversation with her right now."

To his credit he started to stand up, but he immediately sat back down after making eye contact with Arianna.

"You don't need to leave," she said to him. "Whatever you have to say, Auntie, you can say in front of Jiwan."

I was practically overcome by a sarcastic comment but held myself back by sheer force of will. Arianna's statement was straight out of daytime television's version of a relationship, but disagreeing would probably do no good. Besides, there really wasn't time to spare. "If that's how you feel, sure."

I turned to look at this young woman-child, her flowing black hair and angry eyes flashing, and fortified myself to break the news. "You are not returning your mom's calls. You haven't returned my messages. Have you considered that something might be wrong?"

Her cheeks flushed and she clenched her jaw.

"Arianna, I care about you. I'm sitting in Starbucks in a freaking costume because I love you. I think you could give me a minute to tell you why."

Arianna met my eyes, and although she was waiting to hear what I would say, I could tell she was sceptical. Maybe she thought I was going to give her a lecture about right and wrong. And I did want to tell her to be careful with her heart. To not rush. But this wasn't really the time.

Okay, maybe I'd slide it in later on. One-on-one. Yes, that was a wise decision.

I took a deep breath. "Your grandfather is not well. He's

had a heart attack, Arianna. He's at the hospital and I'm here to take you there."

"That's impossible! I just saw him yesterday. He's fine. He was, like, raking the lawn."

I understood I'd caught her off guard, but there was no time for an argument. "Arianna, that is how short life can be. You are raking leaves one day, and your heart is failing the next. We need to go. Now. I have no other information to give you other than it's very serious. You need to be there."

Arianna's skin had gone pale and her hand had flown up to cover her mouth. She'd been preparing for some type of dramatic fight and not a true crisis. I reached out to squeeze her shoulder. "I'm sorry to tell you this way. It's very serious."

"Wow," said Jiwan, reminding us of his presence. He seemed to be short on words of comfort, but he was young and it was forgivable.

"Yes. Wow." I got up from the chair and caught his glance. "Costume party thing," I said in explanation.

I didn't have the slightest idea what they'd been talking about before I arrived – probably something about how terrible their parents were – but that conversation was over. They both stood up and Jiwan reached over to give Arianna an awkward hug across the table. I looked away and headed back out to the car. Arianna followed me.

We drove to the hospital in silence. I knew from experience that if Jas were in the car this would be an ongoing lecture, but that didn't feel like my role. And the way Arianna was cringing in the passenger seat, I thought I knew how she was feeling anyway.

"We'll get there as soon as possible, honey."

She nodded. I dug in my purse and passed her some tissue.

"I should've answered my phone."

"Yes, you should've." I merged onto the freeway. "But it's okay. Sometimes we do things when we're angry or upset without understanding the consequences." I grimaced, thinking back on my own choices this weekend. "It's a learning opportunity."

Arianna snuffled but didn't say anything more.

I wondered what she was thinking, but I didn't want to push her. Instead, I focused on the road. We were coming up on a red light, the last one before the hospital, and I pressed the brake pedal. The mammoth building rose in front of us and, looking up at the hundreds of windows, I wondered if Mr Singh were behind any of them. I turned towards my passenger. "If you need to talk—"

"Why does everyone think I need to talk?"

"Because you are making some adult choices. Besides, everyone needs to talk at some point. I wish I had earlier." The light turned green and I pressed the gas pedal.

Nothing happened.

The driver behind me honked in irritation.

I pressed the pedal again, but still nothing happened. Or at least nothing I wanted it to do happened. The display lights were still on, but the engine faltered, then coughed, then died.

Damn.

I waved frantically for the car behind me to go around and punched on the emergency lights before turning to look at a stunned Arianna.

"What's going on?"

"The damn car's dead! It's out of gas." I didn't bother to explain it was my fault, but that was obvious. Cars did not fill their own gas tanks. "See what I mean about consequences?" Arianna half laughed, half sobbed, and I couldn't blame her. Why was life such a mess?

"I'm just going to flip the hood up, and then we'll run over to the hospital. We've got this. It's under control."

"But...what about the car?"

"It'll probably get towed." Or struck from behind by a driver texting rather than watching the road like an intelligent person. "No big deal."

I carefully opened my car door into the flowing traffic. Pressing my body as close to the vehicle as possible, I managed to manoeuvre my body around the front end without getting killed. I squeezed my fingers under the hood and tried desperately to get the godforsaken metal catch to release. But no luck. I was red-faced, frustrated, and mouthing apologies at annoyed drivers. Except, of course, the guy in the truck who took the time to roll down his window and yell, "Get me some beer, wench!" Him, I gave the finger.

Hallelujah, the lever shifted and the damn hood finally popped open. I could do this. One step at a time. Skirting my way back to the driver's side, I opened the door to more staring and honking before crawling back into my seat.

"Aren't we getting out?" Arianna asked.

"We are. As soon as I get this damn corset off." I'd rather look like a depressed middle-aged goth than a sleazy hussy from the dark ages. "Do you, ah, think you could quickly undo the laces?"

"Wha...?" Arianna giggled through her tears as I wrestled around in my seat so my back faced her. "Oh right. I'd forgotten."

"Unbelievably, so had I."

Arianna made quick work of the laces, and I threw the offending device in the back seat. Taking a deep breath, I let my abdomen expand before reaching for my hooded cape. Might as well layer the homespun. "That's better. Thanks."

I turned back around and faced my goddaughter. Tears were streaming down her face. I pulled her into a hug over the centre console, kissing the top of her head as brakes screeched to a stop behind us. "I love you."

"I love you too, Auntie." Her voice was muffled against my shoulder, but I could understand her. "I'm scared."

"I know. Me too."

Another driver honked, and I was in mortal fear that we'd get rear-ended while still sitting in the vehicle. The traffic light flashed to yellow, then red. We took the opportunity to safely exit the vehicle and cross the road, then ran to the hospital, the sound of my cloak flapping around me.

Chapter Twenty-Nine

Arianna and I arrived at the information desk in a flurry of emotion and sweat. The gracious man behind the desk was quick to direct us to the ICU. Managing to slow ourselves down to a power walk, we made our way through the hospital's maze-like corridors, following the ICU signage until we turned the last corner.

Ahead was a small waiting area with rose-coloured padded chairs; outdated magazines; Mrs Singh, all sari and grey hair piled into a tight bun; and my friend, pacing around the rows of seating.

"Mom!" Arianna cried and dashed towards Jas. Jas caught her daughter and folded her into a hug. I was relieved. Not only had I managed a small miracle – I'd found this well-loved child and gotten her where she needed to be – but, I was pleased to see, they were also both prepared to shelve the argument for the time being.

I collapsed in the chair beside Mrs Singh and tentatively put my arm around her. "I'm so sorry about your husband. Have you any news yet?"

She patted my hand but shook her head. "He's still in surgery. They're giving him something to break the clots. If it works, it will clear his arteries. But…we've not heard anything yet. I hope none of the clots travel to his brain. Or his lungs. They've told us that could happen…"

My throat constricted. I wanted to say something, anything to try and comfort her, but the words were stuck in my throat.

Mrs Singh looked down. "I shouldn't have told him to take care of the yard. It's too much – I…"

"It's not your fault, Mom," Jas interjected. "Dad likes

176

being outside. He likes doing that stuff. He doesn't want to sit around."

"I know, it's just…" Mrs Singh trailed off. She wrapped her arms across her chest and shivered.

There was no telling what would happen to the person she loved, the person she had lived her entire adult life with. It was devastating and I was inept. I looked to Jas for further support, but she'd taken a seat with Arianna, who was talking to her quietly. Looking back at Mrs Singh, the goose flesh standing out on her arms, I gulped down my own insecurities. I needed to be here for her.

"These waiting rooms are always so cold, aren't they, Mrs Singh? The air conditioning is too high." I slipped off my cloak, taking a moment to tug up the tunic that was already slipping down my shoulders. I wrapped the cloak around her shoulders and over her filmy turquoise sari. The woodsy scent of campfire drifted off it, but she smiled in appreciation.

The minutes ticked by and soon it had been an hour. With no new information, we stared down every hospital attendant who walked by. The waiting room filled up with other anxious people waiting to see their loved ones. And slowly, they trickled out, led by one hospital attendant or another, until it was just the four of us once again.

"Why is it taking so long to hear anything?" Arianna voiced our impatience for all of us.

Jas glanced up at the clock for the hundredth time. "I'll go remind the nurse at the triage station if we haven't heard anything in another fifteen minutes, but for now we need to wait. Maybe they are still working on Papa."

"I know." Arianna scuffed her toes on the linoleum in frustration. "But I hate the smell in here," Arianna scrunched her nose as her eyes looked up at the fluorescent lights in disgust. "The chairs are uncomfortable, and it's creepy."

Jas sighed. "Arianna, it's not about you."

"I know that! It's just hospitals suck. Nothing good ever happens in these places. Except babies, I guess." Arianna flushed, her eyes darting towards me and then away, but it was too late. The words were already out. She darted a glance at her mother, then looked at the floor.

In truth, I had a momentary emotional hiccup myself. But I swallowed my old grief, surprised by how telling Arianna's non-verbals were. Had everyone, even Arianna, been tiptoeing around me? I took a deep breath. "It's okay," I said. "You're right. Babies are good things."

A look of sweet relief crossed Arianna's face.

"You do know you can talk about babies around me, right? I'm not going to break." My voice cracked as if trying to betray me, but I ignored it and pushed on. "Honestly."

Jas reached over and squeezed my hand. I could see tears in her eyes and I had to blink rapidly before she set me off. That and change the topic.

"Do you remember that time you busted your wrist tobogganing?" I directed my comment to Arianna. "You were pretty happy about the hospital then."

"But that was because of the popsicles. They gave me like three. I wonder why they give junk food out anyway?"

"To distract children from the smell," interjected Mrs Singh.

The three of us turned to look at her. "What?" she said. "It smells like the inside of a bleach factory in here."

We smiled, momentarily distracted, before lapsing back into our silent vigil. The minutes passed by uncounted until finally someone walked self-assuredly through the 'Personnel only' double doors and approached us. She was in scrubs, a cloth cap covering her hair just like you see on television, and a shiver of fear ran up my spine.

"Mrs Singh?" she asked.

Jas's mother nodded and partially raised her hand in identification. The four of us were seated in a tight huddle, and the woman came over and perched on the edge of a coffee table facing us.

"I'm Dr Chan. Your husband is responding well to the drugs." She paused and smiled reassuringly. "We were able

178

to remove over fifty percent of the blockage. Although he's not out of the woods yet, he's stable, and I'm glad to report that his vitals have not deteriorated further. If you'd like, you can go in and see him. He won't be able to respond, but I'm sure it will be comforting."

Chapter Thirty

As soon as Dr Chan allowed it, the three generations of Singh women left the waiting room to immediately go and visit their papa. Jas was the first one to return, and she almost seemed a different person. Her face, although tired, no longer looked as fractured by stress. I was glad she'd received some comfort in seeing her father, even if he was unconscious.

"Mom and Arianna are going to stay in the recovery room a little longer."

"Well, then, why don't we go down to the cafeteria and pick up some tea for everyone," I suggested. Jas agreed and we made our way back downstairs.

"I can't thank you enough for finding Arianna and bringing her here. I was beside myself – completely sick with worry – and I couldn't handle one more thing. My dad…" she shook her head and bit her lip. "And my mother. She's never even lived alone."

I listened as Jas talked. There was no other way to support her but be present.

After ordering and paying for our tea, I tried to distract her with a complete play-by-play of the Arianna mission, including the telephone recon, Starbucks crackdown and car fiasco. I'd have to do something about that before too long, or it would be towed. Then Jas got me up to speed on receiving her mother's panicked phone call and her race down to the hospital.

Apparently there'd been some delay in my responding to her texts. In the time it had taken me to turn my phone on and receive the texts, Jas had asked someone else for assistance in finding Arianna.

"I'm so dumb. I actually asked Daniel for help."

I turned and looked at Jas, my shock written in capital letters across my face. She asked yoga guy – hello, had they not just met? – for assistance with her daughter! I thought better of saying anything and took a sip of my tea instead.

"Yup, he's an idiot." She crossed her arms in agitation. "He apparently doesn't believe teenage sex is a big deal. Thinks I should relax. Can you believe someone with no kids thinks they should be giving advice on parenting?"

I cringed. I knew she wasn't talking about me, but still.

Jas bit her lip. "Sorry. I didn't mean it that way. He's just so opinionated. And it's not as if I'd asked his opinion in the first place. It's definitely not going to work. Maybe, you know, if I didn't have Arianna, I wouldn't care so much. Perhaps his body might be enough."

I spluttered on my tea and we both laughed. Perhaps it was the stress feeding into our nerves, but it felt good.

When I finally managed to speak, I said, "He does have a nice body."

Jas nodded. "It's excellent."

"Did you ever...?" I ventured.

"Mm-hmm." Jas swallowed some of her own tea while I started to hyperventilate. "As you know, it's high time for me to start living again."

"Holy shit!" That was about all I could muster. "That must've been...exciting."

"Like I said, body is fantastic, brain is missing."

"So...you're okay, then? Just a one-time thing, and now what?"

Jas didn't answer right away. I realised it was a stupid question to have asked. The future would be impacted by how much support her parents – or parent – would need. But after all this time alone, it was exciting to think Jas might consider being in an intimate relationship again.

"For now, I keep taking care of the people who are important to me" – a wide grin spread across her face – "and that includes taking care of me. The truth is, I miss the company of a man in my life." I smiled back. Whatever happened, I knew my friend was tough and could manage the competing demands. "But what about you?" Any insights after your adventurous weekend?"

"Oh. Right. Thanks for reminding me." I took a sip of my tea as I thought about what I wanted to say. I'd successfully pushed the whole larp experience onto the back-burner. The search for Arianna had been a great way to help me avoid thinking about the painful words Ralph and I had churned out in the tent. I shifted in my chair. "I'm processing still. It was," I struggled to find the words, "more than I expected."

"Did you find out... Was he...?"

I wrinkled my brow. "Was he? Oh! No," I managed to chuckle despite my painful jealousy, as I remembered the fevered texts I'd sent Jas from the embankment above the headquarters. "The short answer is no." I took a deep breath to steady my voice. I was quickly becoming the emotional equivalent of a metronome. "It's just, not been the same between us. Since, you know. Since we lost the baby. The whole thing...it's become this splinter between Ralph and me and neither of us seems to know how to get rid of it." I blinked rapidly and focused my attention to methodically destroying the corrugated sleeve I had removed from my disposable cup. "Man! I'm a complete mess."

"Tell me about it." Jas reached over and squeezed my arm.

"Can't hide anything from you, can I?"

"Nope." Jas gave me a few minutes to collect myself. Perhaps she thought I was done. But I surprised the crap out of her – and my damn self – when I continued.

"It makes sense now. This whole larp thing. You can kind of immerse yourself in this alternate reality and put aside what's happening in the real world. Escape for a bit. Not that it makes it better, it's just, I kind of get it now."

Jas nodded. "So does that mean you and Ralph left on good terms then?"

"Hell no!"

Again we snickered before falling into a comfortable

silence. Until I remembered the damn car.

"I guess I'm going to have to call Ralph about the car. Maybe he can bring a jerry can or something." I grimaced at the thought. I wasn't sure I was ready for direct communication yet. But I'd need to do something about the vehicle, or perhaps the city had already towed it to the impound lot.

"You could try Bendar. I think he lives around here."

I looked up at my friend. "Bendar?"

"You know, we met him at Dad's party."

"Right, I know who Bendar is. But, pray tell, how do *you* know where he lives? Forgive me if I'm wrong, but don't you detest him?" It had been only a week or so since the night they'd attended the orchestra performance, and unless I'd dreamt it all, it had been sorely uncomfortable.

Jas had the decency to blush. "Remember when Mom said we had lots in common? Turns out we work for the same company – he transferred from the Vancouver office. He's a corporate accountant. Small world, hey?"

"So basically your mom wasn't trying to set you up?" Jas shrugged her shoulder in response. "How did you find this out, anyway?"

"Through a rather awkward encounter in the elevator last week. I meant to tell you, but…you know. You had a lot going on."

Had I? The truth was, I'd had nothing much going on in my life for a long time, but a lot going on in my head. I wondered if this happened often – occurrences in Jas's life she didn't tell me about because of my mental and emotional preoccupation with my own life.

"He's actually a really nice guy. I regret I was such a jerk when I met him, but second chances, you know? We've actually met up a few times for a walk during our lunch break."

"So…" I said, choosing my words carefully. "Are you perhaps interested, then?"

Jas smiled. "In friendship maybe. Did I forget to mention? He's gay, Gill."

I raised my eyebrows.

"He told me after we'd met up a few times. It's a big part of the reason he moved here. Fresh start. It can be tough in my community, breaking new ground. I should know."

I nodded in a bit of a fog. "Right. So he lives near here?"

"I think so… I'll just send a text and see if he can help with the car. Unless you'd rather try Ralph?" She looked at me questioningly.

"Nope! That's okay. He probably hasn't made it back to town yet anyway. Let's try Bendar." Sure, I was avoiding the inevitable, but I could hide under the excuse a little while longer. I leaned back in my chair and closed my eyes as Jas sent a text off to Bendar. I couldn't help the smile that stretched across my face as the pieces fell into place. No wonder he was tired of being set up with women.

Here we were, each of us living our own private struggles. Were we really any different? Probably not.

"Let's take this tea back, before it gets cold." We exited the cafeteria and returned to the ICU waiting room, each carrying an extra cup of tea. We found the women huddled together in the otherwise deserted space, Arianna's arm resting on Mrs Singh's back. The elderly woman seemed incredibly small and frail. Not at all the feisty lady who had hosted dozens of guests in her home just a few weeks earlier.

"Any changes?" Jas asked. Her mother and daughter both shook their heads. "That's okay. It's what they told us to expect, remember? He's stable for now." We set their tea down on a table. Jas leaned over to give her family a group hug and Mrs Singh started weeping. From fear or from relief at seeing her husband alive, I couldn't say. But either way, the sound was heart-wrenching and my own throat closed with emotion.

I blinked my eyes rapidly, trying to stop my own tears from falling. This was a private moment. A time for family to be together. I stood up, ready to walk to the restroom and give them a few minutes, when Mrs Singh let go of her daughter and granddaughter and motioned for me to come to her.

I walked over, hesitation in my step. I wasn't comfortable with emotional pain at the best of times. I never knew the right thing to say or do. But it turned out that didn't matter. Mrs Singh, Arianna, and then Jas put their arms around me, and suddenly we were in a quadruple hug. A hug of sadness and of hope and of solidarity. Of not knowing what the future held, but knowing we had each other.

It was nearing midnight, and for the most part the hospital was quiet around us. I'd met Bendar at my forsaken car a few hours before; he'd thankfully not commented on my clothing choice. But without the corset, my tunic really looked more potato sack than anything else.

We'd emptied one jerry can of gas into the tank, and I'd driven directly to a gas station to top it up before returning to the hospital. Our waiting room vigil had continued for a few more hours, and it was apparent to me that Mrs Singh, as tired and worn as she seemed, was not leaving anytime soon.

"Would you like me to take Arianna home? I could stay with her the night and bring her back in the morning? Or after school?"

Jas was about to answer, but she stopped herself and turned to her daughter. "Arianna? What do you think is the better option for you – staying here or going home with Gill?" I could see her biting her tongue, wanting to add more, and I was proud of her when she didn't.

Arianna's brow furrowed. "What if something happens? And I'm not here?"

"I will call you if anything changes. But it's your choice."

Arianna looked around the deserted waiting room; I imagined her mentally weighing the options. "I'm coming back in the morning."

"Right," Jas said and nodded. I half expected her to mention school, but she didn't. "Of course."

Chapter Thirty-One

"Auntie," whispered Arianna, "are you awake?" We lay side by side in Jas's queen-sized bed. It had been Arianna's suggestion we both sleep there, just like the sleepovers we'd had when she was younger. I'd agreed nonchalantly, not wanting to make too big a deal of it. I figured we were both feeling nostalgic and in need of support tonight. Once I'd lain down, I'd immediately started drifting off. The weekend of sleepless nights and the emotional weight of the day had caught up with me.

"Just barely. What's up?"

"Do you think Papa will...die?"

I was alert in seconds. How was a person supposed to answer a question like that? The easy road, assuring her he'd be fine, seemed disingenuous. Besides, the outcome was completely out of my hands. I took a gulp of air and tentatively began looking for the right words. "Honestly, honey, I don't know." Okay, zero percent inspirational, but it was at least truthful. "He doesn't seem to be getting any worse at this point, which is good. Your grandfather takes good care of his health and stays active. But this...I just don't know." I reached over and held her hand, giving her fingers a squeeze.

There were no guarantees in life. I was thinking about Keith, and I'd have been surprised if she wasn't thinking of her father also. I wondered how much she remembered of their life before he died or of the accident, but I didn't ask and let her direct the conversation instead. Besides, I wasn't exactly an expert at this. What if I said the wrong thing?

"Do you think, sometimes, people die before they're supposed to?"

"What do you mean?"

"I mean Dad."

Right. So she was thinking of Keith. I flashed back to the moment I'd heard of the accident. Or hadn't heard. Because I hadn't answered the phone. I'd been in the laundry room, sorting lights from darks and delicates from jeans, and although I'd heard the phone ring, I hadn't raced to answer it, thinking that if it was important, they'd leave a message.

When the incessant ringing stopped and then started again, I'd rolled my eyes. It was likely a telemarketer. Or Ralph's senile aunt from the coast. Calling to tell me about her cats again. I'd again dismissed the call.

Later I'd found out it had been Jas. The call announcing Keith's death. Killed in a moment, in a head-on collision while driving the family minivan. He'd left work early to pick up Arianna at school. But he'd never made it. Had instead been T-boned by a truck running a red light and that was it. Dead at thirty-four; unquestionably too early.

My free hand rested on my empty uterus. "You know, honey, life isn't fair. That's the truth of it. Not everyone gets a fair shake. Things happen. Miserable things happen. They don't always make sense. So you've got to go for it while you have a chance. Make your life what you want it to be. Cause we just never know how long we have."

Maybe the problem was I'd given up on my marriage. If I was honest, then I'd admit I'd held back key pieces of the equation in my discussions with Dr Torres. If I truly wanted to move forwards, I'd have to find the courage to lay those pieces on that damn glass table of hers.

I filed that uncomfortable thought away for later. Right now it was more important that I was present for Arianna. "Your dad lived that way."

The pillow rustled underneath Arianna's head, and I could hear, rather than see, her turn in my direction. "He did?"

"Oh ya. He didn't let anything stop him. Not culture. Not expectations. Not what everyone else thought was right. He wanted to be with your mom even though everyone else

187

said it wouldn't work. A Catholic and a Sikh? That just didn't happen. Still doesn't, that often. But they were happy and they loved each other. And of course there was you. You were a little miracle too."

"What do you mean?"

"I just remember Keith holding you, your fuzzy black hair peeking out of the blanket, and he said, 'This baby is amazing. No rational person would choose to miss out on this child.' And you know what? He was right. There was no way your Papa was going to miss out on your life. You brought them together, your grandfather and your dad, and I, for one, hadn't been sure that would ever happen. But you did it. You made it happen."

I squeezed her hand. I loved this girl so much.

"You know, honey," I said, not knowing if this was the right timing but rushing on before I could change my mind. "Your dad was awesome. And your parents were great together. I think that's why your mom hasn't been in a rush to find anyone else. I know you think she should date, that if she had her own life she wouldn't be so involved in yours. But I doubt it. Your mom's not like that. She's always going to have an opinion, and she's always going to fight for what she sees as your best interest. If I had a girl as wonderful as you, I'd be in your face, too."

"Do you think mom'll be alone for ever? Cause I've been thinking about it, and it'll probably weird me out if she starts dating. But…it might help her understand better, too, you know? That I want to date and it's okay to be interested in guys."

"Maybe." I didn't exactly know what the future held for them. I pictured a double date in my head but quickly swallowed my amusement. "Your mom will start dating when she's ready. But I do believe she's getting there." Although, if Mr Singh passed away, Jas would probably be busy taking care of her mother and dating might again be forced into the back seat. Lately I'd been envious of the excitement that came with single status. But it could be hard work too. And just as lonely.

"She's really pissed at me right now."

"About Jiwan? I doubt it. She was just surprised. And mad that you'd lied to her."

"But I can't tell her the truth. She's so reactive!"

I chuckled. "Ya, she is. Sounds like a girl I ran into at Starbucks today."

"Ha. Very funny."

We stopped talking, and eventually Arianna's breath evened out into the gentle rhythm of sleep. I listened to the beautiful sound for a while, wondering what amazing things she would do in her life.

Eventually, with feather-light movements, I eased off the bed and out the room. I couldn't put the task off any longer.

I picked up my phone and made the call. It rang unanswered three times. Four. Maybe he'd left the phone in the car? Or maybe he could see the phone where it sat ringing, could see my name and number flashing and was choosing not to pick up. I took a deep breath, already planning out what message I'd leave on his voice mail.

"Hello?"

"Oh, hi," I said, stumbling over my words. "I thought it was going to voicemail."

"I was unpacking – got to it just in time. Where are you?"

"I'm staying at Jas's tonight—"

"Gillian, come home. We need to talk."

"I can't, actually." I cleared my throat. "It's Mr Singh. He's had a heart attack."

There was a pause as Ralph processed what I'd said. "Oh no! Is he okay?"

"They're not sure yet. He's still at the hospital. But the doctor did say he was stable when I left about an hour ago. Jas is still there with her mom. I've brought Arianna home and am going to spend the night with her here."

"Right. That's a good idea." The silence stretched between us. I didn't want to hang up, but I didn't know what to say. "Let me know if you hear anything more about Mr Singh."

I promised him I would, then hung up the phone and lay back down beside Arianna. A tear trickled down from the corner of my eye and wet the hair at my temples.

Life was rarely fair.

Chapter Thirty-Two

Rosie took the rented wench garments out of the bag and carefully laid them across her sales counter for a close examination of buttons, cuffs and seams. Finding everything in order (I'd washed out the grass stain with tent-flashback remorse and elbow grease early that morning), she leaned over the counter, a sweet smile on her face. All traces of the sledgehammer-wielding elf had been erased and the innocent granny had returned.

"Did you discover what you set out to find, dear?"

Had I? "In a way, I suppose. But then, you know... I'm not sure what I found was really what I wanted." I was talking in circles. But this little old lady – orange lips by weekday, green skin by weekend – was probably okay with that kind of communication. She nodded gravely, as though what I'd said made the slightest sense. I smiled and felt gratified; it was as though someone understood me, and I almost reached over the counter and gave her a hug. I had a soft spot for this elderly eccentric; she'd assaulted me, sure, and yet I appreciated her ferocity.

Rosie handed me my rental contract with *Paid in Full* stamped across it. "I can't say I'm surprised."

"Pardon?" I asked. Something about her statement caught my attention. "What do you mean, you aren't surprised?"

Rosie used her knobbly elbows to hoist herself up on the bar stool behind the counter. She took her time getting comfortable, arranging her flowing sequinned skirt before responding. "Well, dear, you just don't have the look of an observer about you."

"Oh?" I smiled. "And what kind of look do I have?" I

wouldn't have been surprised if Rosie had pulled a deck of tarot cards out from a drawer and started reading my fortune. You could say she had that kind of look to her. That, and a general quirkiness. I leaned in over the glass counter, its contents filled with costume jewellery, skull coffee mugs, and assorted fake eyelash sets.

Rosie shook her bejewelled fist in my face. "You have the look of someone who grabs life by the bullocks and shakes out what she wants."

Oh, jeez. Cow balls! I pulled my head back at the unappetizing visual, but I laughed.

"And that kind of person," she said, "is never going to be happy standing at the sidelines as a non-player character. You've gotta be all in. Or all out." She lowered her fist to the counter.

The silence stretched between us as a wave of acceptance flooded my heart; I knew Rosie was right. All in or all out. None of this *half way is good enough*. It did not bring the kind of marriage I wanted to be in. Sometimes compromise costs too much.

I stuck my hand out and Rosie shook it. Her skin loosely covered her feather-light bones, and it amazed me that so much life could feel so frail. "I've really enjoyed meeting you, Rosie. You are a scholar and a gentle lady...and a tough old broad too." I rubbed my chest where her sledgehammer had pounded me. I felt sad that our paths were not likely to cross again. "I, um, imagine you have a fist full of balls yourself."

Rosie grinned. "You bet your ass I do."

I made my way outside, the dingle of the bells on the door announcing my emergence into the light. As the sunlight flooded the sky and street around me, I stopped and let it warm my skin. It seemed the finest light I'd felt in a long while. Alone or with Ralph, I was going to grab life and shake.

There was no point racing home to a household full of memories and ruining my new outlook. And I didn't want to bother Jas. She was at home taking a much-needed rest. Her mother, having still refused to leave the hospital, now had her granddaughter for support and company. I'd dropped Arianna off this morning, before attending a short work meeting and picking up the compositions I'd need to practise for the coming season.

With nothing else to do, I drove in the direction of the yoga studio even though my class wouldn't begin for two hours. Time on my own seemed a good idea; I'd spend it at the café located conveniently across the street from yoga.

I ordered tea and a Mediterranean salad with grilled chicken. Waiting for my food, I looked around at all the happy couples conversing, the colleagues discussing ideas over paperwork, and the harried parents trying to persuade toddlers to eat, to stay silent, to not throw packets of sugar on the floor. When I was younger, I would have been horrified to eat alone.

But what was horrible about it? Between my peppermint tea and me, it was refreshingly agony-free. There was no pretending. No overwhelming hostility. No "too angry to speak" or "too angry to listen." And even better, the rejection that came with the "I'm more interested in my phone or the newspaper than you" was also happily missing.

It hadn't always been that way. But it was the reality of what our marriage had become. Was it inevitable? Of its own accord, my hand groped at the dragonfly pendant around my neck. Had we made the mistake of transforming in the wrong direction? It was impossible to return to who we'd been before, but was it possible to continue changing into something else? Did marriage mean having to stay stuck in the same patterns?

As I waited for my salad, I people-watched, and I allowed myself not to feel self-conscious about being alone. So what if I didn't have kids? So what if I didn't have a partner? I might be happier this way.

A couple sat in the booth next to me. I could've stared at them for twenty minutes and I don't think they would've noticed. They were each engrossed in what the other was saying, both totally engaged in the context of whatever they were discussing (which happened to be an upcoming holiday to Spain, the price of a rental car, and whether the GPS would be in Spanish or English – hey, voices carry in those kinds of public places; it wasn't as though I was purposely eavesdropping. It just sort of happened).

That was what I wanted in life. Not the trip to Spain (although it sounded fantastic; I started wondering how many travel points I had racked up). It was the companionship. It had been a long time since Ralph and I had been like that.

That day in my kitchen, Jas had been right: It wasn't the larp that had changed things between Ralph and me. It hadn't caused our problems; it had only revealed them. And one day I might have it in me to be grateful for the whole crazy weekend I'd just experienced. But not yet. It was still a teensy bit too fresh.

My salad arrived, and as I ate, I continued to watch the people around me. Especially the couples. Who was speaking and who wasn't. Who was complacent and who had given up. I felt as if I could see what was going on, even if they couldn't see it.

And it wasn't just Jas who'd been right, it was Rosie too. Life was over before you knew it. It was time to grab life by the proverbial balls and shake the shit out of it. I wasn't going to stay on the sidelines any longer. I didn't know exactly what that would mean for the future, but I knew I had to move in a different direction if I wanted to be happy. If a dragonfly could move in six directions, then I could too.

But it needed to be the right direction and not just a distraction from the truth. As if a kitchen could fill the empty space inside a person. Inside a home.

I glanced back at the couple who were so enamored with each other. Had they only started dating a short time ago? Or had they been together for years? I couldn't tell by their ages, and I'd at first assumed it was a newer relationship based on their mutual interest for what the other had to say. But maybe it was possible they'd been together for some time.

Maybe long marriages could be passionate and full of connection and neither Ralph nor I needed to settle for less. But whether ours could be that kind of marriage…that was a question I didn't have an answer to.

Chapter Thirty-Three

After paying my bill, I retrieved my yoga mat from the car and made my way to the studio. It was twenty minutes before class, and I appeared to be one of the first students there. I rolled my mat out in my favourite location under the cold air return and gathered what props I may have needed. Then I lay down on my mat, with a bolster under my knees, my eyes closed, and my arms stretched out in surrender as new participants quietly joined me in the studio.

Someone squeezed my shoulder. I opened an eye, and sure enough, it was Jas.

"Hi, honey," she whispered in greeting.

"Hey. Aren't you supposed to be home, getting some rest?"

"I'm too keyed up. I'm hoping yoga might help burn off some of my tension."

I watched her set out her mat and props beside me, waiting till she was lying on her mat before asking how her dad was doing.

"He opened his eyes this morning. Squeezed my hand. He's very weak but peaceful."

"That's good."

"It is," Jas agreed. We both closed our eyes and relaxed while we could. Soon enough the teacher would have us sweating as we ran through several sun salutations.

I sensed someone come in and take the empty spot on my right. It sounded as though they were fumbling around with their equipment, but I didn't open my eyes until I heard the teacher tap her tiny cymbal and welcome everyone to practice.

I slowly rolled over to my side in order to push myself

up to a seated position.

"Ralph?" I said. Was I seeing things? The person who had made a commotion setting up their mat beside me was none other than my husband. A man who hadn't ever shown the slightest interest in yoga, other than buying me a new mat one year for Christmas.

"Hi," he said and ran his fingers through his hair. "Did I do this right?" A giant heap lay in front of him with every imaginable prop the studio kept.

The instructor had started to greet the class and I whispered back, "*What* are you doing here?"

Ralph looked sheepishly around the room. He seemed a bit nervous in his joggers and Blue Jays T-shirt. As he should be. This was not a beginner class. "Yoga?" he said.

The rest of the class was moving into a seated half lotus, and I moved into position. Ralph watched me and used his arms to try and manoeuvre his legs into a similar arrangement. The instructor had started a visualization exercise and the other participants were silent all around us.

"I just thought," Ralph whispered, "I just thought I would, you know, give it a try. I know it's something you really like." The woman in front of us turned her head and gave Ralph a dirty look, but being new to yoga, he probably didn't realise that being quiet wasn't acceptable when you were supposed to be silent. "I love you, Gillian."

I didn't need to look in the mirror to know my expression was one of bewilderment. I nodded. "Okay. Yes. Well. Have fun?" I closed my eyes and did my best meditation fake.

But I couldn't help looking out of the corner of my eye at Jas. She was looking out of the corner of her eye at me, biting her lip with eyebrows raised.

Chapter Thirty-Four

When class ended, I peeled Ralph off the floor.

"Tired?" I asked.

He nodded before rolling up his borrowed mat and placing it and the plethora of props back in the cupboard. Jas suggested Ralph take Advil and a hot bath when he got home. He nodded agreement and we both gave her a fond farewell. She was headed back to the hospital.

"Call me if you need any help," I said.

Ralph had taken the train from work, so we walked out to my car in an awkward silence. We were, for the first time since the painful tent episode, alone.

I fumbled through my purse for my keys, the wind swirling my hair and cooling my skin. The sky had clouded over since I'd entered the studio and I could smell the coming rain. My fingers curled around my keychain at last and I pulled them out.

"You were right." I could sense Ralph turning his eyes on me but kept my own vision trained on the café I'd eaten in earlier. "You were right about a lot of things. Maybe I haven't grieved properly." My heart felt curiously thawed after the longest of emotional winters.

Ralph reached over and squeezed my shoulder. I didn't move and he let his hand fall back to his side. "It was dumb of me. What I said. In the tent. I shouldn't have, Gill. I was...I was just angry. I'm sorry."

"Don't be sorry. You should've said it a long time ago." The cold wind blew through my yoga pants. I stamped my feet lightly on the asphalt of the parking lot and shrugged. "Although I'm not sure I'd have been ready to hear you." I looked up, a lopsided half grin on my face. "Guess it took roleplaying for me to finally face reality."

Ralph nodded. "Life deals out shit sometimes, you know? Sometimes it's nice to escape."

I turned away and leaned my back against our Camry. My fingers were tracing the sharp edges of my car key over and over in a kind of therapeutic mantra. It was soothing, the ridges and valleys against my fingertips.

"My freaking back and shoulders are killing me already," said Ralph, coming to lean up against the car beside me. "What the hell was that?"

I laughed. "Downward dog? Plank? Or maybe it was the headstands? It gets easier. Maybe try a beginner class next time."

He grunted.

"It was a nice thing to do. Coming here, trying my thing."

The wind smarted my face and dried my tears before they could fall. I again ran my fingers over the key's jagged edge and took a deep breath. It was now. Because if it wasn't now, it might be never. "Can you take me?" I swallowed hard. "I mean, would you go with me? Because I've never been."

Ralph nodded. I passed him the keys and we got in my car. He adjusted the driver's seat, buckled up, and started the vehicle before looking over at me.

"You're sure?"

I nodded.

We drove with the music off and the heat on, the forced air warming my face and cold hands. The rain started to fall. It slid down the windows in teardrops, the windshield wipers moving back and forth, counting out the seconds like a metronome. With rush hour all but over, it took no time at all before we were parking in the half-deserted lot.

My heart pounded. This was it. I swallowed my fear, as much as I could, and got out of the car, not waiting for Ralph but trusting him to follow. I started walking, one foot in front of the other. *Don't think. Just do.* For once, my heart was open. I was ready.

"Gill, he's not by Keith."

It took a minute for Ralph's words to register. I turned around and faced him. He was still standing beside my car, on the other side of the parking lot.

"He's over this way." Ralph pointed to a path I hadn't noticed. It looped between two giant elms then twisted off in a direction I couldn't see. I flushed and walked back, feeling the weight of insufficiency already. Maybe I should just get back in the car. Maybe I wasn't ready. Coming here wouldn't change the past.

But as I reached out to open the door handle, Ralph enveloped my cold hand in his. "Come on, let me show you." I looked up and Ralph's gaze held mine. Could I do this? Could I trust Ralph that I was ready for this? I was sure he could feel my erratic pulse through his fingertips.

"Please, Gillian."

Ralph turned, and I did not pull my hand from his grasp. Together we slowly entered the path that meandered between the giant elms. The rain-dampened shale crunched underfoot and broke the silence, and droplets fell off the leaves and settled in my hair.

Manicured flowerbeds joined the towering trees that lined our path. Our progress was so slow, I was able to take in each flower. There were tulips, the spring bulbs having been the first to force their way out from the earth. The bright red and yellow blossoms stood out against the green foliage, and we continued forward, step by step.

Ahead I could see an open grove. And just coming into view, a large winged statue. An angel was standing atop a marble plinth, and in her arms, she held a small child.

My feet stopped moving. My heart was racing and I was almost panting. Although the humid air was entering my lungs, it didn't seem to be providing me enough oxygen. I was panicking. Was I ready for this?

But Ralph held my hand more firmly and pulled me forward, step after step. I kept my eyes focused on the statue that stood in the centre of the green. Because if I focused on the statue, then I did not have to see the memorial wall snaking along behind it. I kept my feet moving, one step in front of the other. Each step a decision to stay the course.

Until, at last, we stood in front of the statue. A resting child in the open arms of an angel. The infant was still. Stone still. I did not need to touch it to know it was cold. Lifeless yet beautiful. Eventually I dropped my eyes to read the inscription at the statue's base:

Sleeping Angel's Grove
Little One,
You were loved, are loved, will be loved.
In life, in death, and in memory.

Several minutes passed before Ralph turned and continued on the path, still gripping my cold hand in his warm one. We were now walking towards the stone memorial wall ahead. From this distance, I could see the hard granite was embedded with small rectangular plaques. Although we were still too far away to read the engravings, I knew what I would find there.

I continued walking, my body shaking, tears silently trailing down my face. I used my sleeve to wipe them. I'd never come. In all this time, I'd never come here. I had to stop. My feet did not want to move.

"Look at me," I said with a shaky laugh. "I'm a mess. And I barely knew him."

"But you loved him."

It was true. I had loved him, had waited for him for so long. But the outcome – it was something I hadn't been prepared for. Even with months knowing what the very probable outcome would be, I had not accepted it in my heart.

"I wanted to be a mom."

"I know."

Without the sound of our footfalls on the shale path, silence surrounded us. I didn't know how that could be, because wasn't life continuing all around us? Weren't squirrels out scavenging and shouldn't birds be nattering at each other? Cars must be travelling through nearby streets and the people in those cars must be deciding what to have for dinner, sharing the events of the day. But here, in the grove, was silence.

I wondered how often people visited this resting space. Did it bring peace, or did it reawaken loss? The memorial wall stretched on and on and I could not count the number of individual markers.

"Okay," I said. "I'm ready." We resumed walking and Ralph led me to a bench half way down the wall.

"Right here, Gillian." He pointed to a particular plaque not five steps from us. It looked, from this distance, no different from the rest. I stood up, placing one foot in front of the other until I could reach out and touch the engraving, feel the indentations with my fingertips.

Zachary Campbell.

Our baby.

My tears fell, and they freed me as they did. Life could not be the same. But it wouldn't just pass by anymore either. I knew that now. I could choose a new direction and transform. I wouldn't be sitting on the sidelines. I'd grab life and shake, until whatever goodness it had in store for me poured out.

THE END

Author's Note

I first learned about Trisomy 18 in much the same way that Gillian did, from a pamphlet while pregnant with my first child in 2006. I read that Trisomy 18 (sometimes known as Edwards Syndrome) was not compatible with life.

While it is truth that the infant mortality rate for children with Trisomy 18 is extremely high, some children do live. About 10% will see their first birthdays.

To learn more about Trisomy 18 or to get connected with online support, contact: The Trisomy 18 Foundation: **http://www.trisomy18.org/**

Fantastic Books
Great Authors

CROOKED
CAT

Meet our authors and discover
our exciting range:

- Gripping Thrillers
- Cosy Mysteries
- Romantic Chick-Lit
- Fascinating Historicals
- Exciting Fantasy
- Young Adult and Children's
  Adventures

Visit us at:
www.crookedcatpublishing.com

Join us on facebook:
www.facebook.com/crookedcatpublishing

CPSIA information can be obtained
at www.ICGtesting.com
Printed in the USA
LVOW12s1544230117
521874LV00003B/838/P